A PUFFIN BOOK

PROPERTY OF

_____

_____

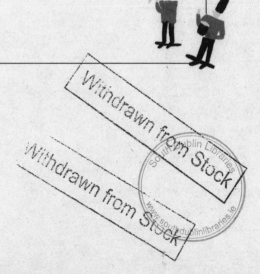

Withdrawn from Stock

Withdrawn from Stock

South Dublin Libraries

www.southdublinlibraries.ie

D1078601

PENELOPE FARMER was born in Kent, in 1939, the younger of twin girls. After attending boarding school and Oxford University, she did a variety of jobs, from teaching to working as a filing clerk, followed by a year of social studies at London University. Then she settled down to raise a family and write full time – including nine novels and many other shorter stories for children, and five novels for adults.

Withdrawn from Stock

# PENELOPE FARMER

# CHARLOTTE SOMETiMES

Illustrated by Chris Connor

PUFFIN BOOKS

UK | USA | Canada | Ireland | Australia
India | New Zealand | South Africa

Puffin Books is part of the Penguin Random House group of companies
whose addresses can be found at global.penguinrandomhouse.com.

www.penguin.co.uk
www.puffin.co.uk
www.ladybird.co.uk

First published by Chatto and Windus 1969
Reissued in this edition 2019

001

Text copyright © Penelope Farmer, 1969, 1985
Revised edition copyright © William and Charlotte Rayner, 1992
Illustrations by Chris Connor

The moral right of the author and illustrator has been asserted

Set in 12.5/16.5 pt Sabon LT Std
Typeset by Jouve (UK), Milton Keynes
Printed and bound in Great Britain by Clays Ltd, Elcograf S.p.A.

A CIP catalogue record for this book is available from the British Library

ISBN: 978-0-141-37921-0

All correspondence to:
Puffin Books
Penguin Random House Children's
80 Strand, London WC2R 0RL

Penguin Random House is committed to a
sustainable future for our business, our readers
and our planet. This book is made from Forest
Stewardship Council® certified paper.

# PART ONE

# CHAPTER ONE

B Y bedtime all the faces, the voices had blurred for Charlotte to one face, one voice. She prepared herself for bed, very slowly and deliberately, cleaning her teeth with the new green toothbrush, undressing awkwardly because she did not like to hide herself in the washing cubicle with her fellow new girl, Susannah; but she was on the other hand much too shy and strange to undress as openly as the other three, Vanessa, Janet and Elizabeth. Vanessa wandered about for ten minutes at least in just her vest and navy-blue school knickers. She had freckles all over her legs. Charlotte had never seen anyone with freckled legs before.

Susannah had ceased chattering which was a relief, but still giggled whenever Janet and Vanessa did, though she could not possibly have heard what they were giggling about. Janet and Vanessa talked, or rather whispered, exclusively to each other. The fourth girl, Elizabeth, was sprawled on her bed, reading a book. Charlotte had a book beside her too, but was so tired and confused she did not want to open it now. Her eyes felt stretched and huge. The light seemed too bright for them, glaring on white walls, white sheets and bed covers; even the polished brown linoleum seemed to shine too much, so that the darkness when the light went out was thankful and cooling.

'Pull the blind up, Charlotte,' a voice ordered – Vanessa's probably, but it might have been Janet's. Charlotte had to climb to the end of her bed to do that and, the blind speeding up with a hiss, saw the moon rising across the river, a huge September hunter's moon, the colour, almost the texture, of honey.

At first, though so tired, she could not sleep. Her bed was uncomfortable in an unfamiliar way. Her old-fashioned school nightdress felt heavy and hot. All the sounds about her were unfamiliar, from the smothering roars of the aeroplanes to the slither of feet in the passages outside. She heard whispers and giggles from Janet and Vanessa, little snores from Elizabeth, the odd sob from Susannah. She found herself worrying about her own younger sister Emma, whom she had left behind alone at home. After a while she began to think it might be a relief if she could cry as Susannah was doing, so perhaps cry herself to sleep, but she could not cry – her eyes felt quite dried up. Every time too, that her eyelids dropped an aeroplane came and jerked her awake again.

She must have slept at last, for later she awoke, abruptly, confusedly. At first she thought another aeroplane must have woken her, racing its engines as it neared the airport. But the silence seemed somehow too complete for that. The moon was silver now and bright, high in the sky. The shadows of the window bars lay on the foot of her bed, and beyond the window she thought she saw a tree, a huge tree, black against the light, but silver where the moon caught, with foliage like thick floating strokes across its trunk. Yet it was odd, for as she became more awake she remembered there was no tree, only a red brick arm jutting out from the main school building where she lay. Sleepily, she took it for some mere trick of light, of the deceptive moon, and fell asleep again, though she dreamed all night in muddled snatches of the day that had just gone, her first day at boarding school.

There were four pillars at the entrance to the school, making a portico that looked grander than the building. Four steps led up to double wooden doors with brass handles on them – their little flash and gleam in the morning sun had been almost the first thing Charlotte saw as she drove in through the gates in the white school bus, among a great many other girls all wearing the same dark-blue uniform as she wore herself. She looked perhaps more primly organized than most, the pleats in her skirt very sharp and new, but felt hopelessly dazed and strange. In the rush to get out when the bus drew up she had scarcely dared to move until she heard suddenly over the jumble of voices her own name loudly called.

'Charlotte Makepeace, Charlotte *Makepeace*!'

'Yes,' Charlotte said shyly. 'Yes,' again, more loudly, and a tall fair girl much older than herself grabbed the case from her hand and led her out of the bus and crowd and noise, through the portico, up still empty stairs.

'I'm Sarah,' she said over her shoulder. 'I'm taking you to your bedroom.' Otherwise she said nothing, walking ahead all the way along miles of indecipherable passages and eventually down four steep steps. She had a curious walk, Charlotte noticed, as if with each step ropes were slackened in her and then pulled tight again. Perhaps this was because she was so tall.

The bedroom to which she took Charlotte had the name *Cedar* printed on a small blue card pinned to its door. All the bedrooms were called after trees it seemed. There was nothing here to suggest particularly a cedar tree, though through the window Charlotte could see other kinds of trees. She saw also a corner of the river, the view cut off sharply by the jutting of the building on the right.

In the room were five black iron bedsteads like Charlotte's own at her home, Aviary Hall. They were about as chipped and shabby too, but had white cotton bedspreads on them, smooth as snow. There were five white chests-of-drawers and five white-painted chairs, and across one corner a faded curtain hung on an iron rod to make the washing cubicle.

'Which bed do you want, Charlotte?' the tall girl Sarah asked, dumping Charlotte's case down on one of the chests-of-drawers.

'Which am I allowed?' asked Charlotte falteringly. The bed nearest the window she saw had little wheels with ornamented spokes on them like wagon wheels where the others had ordinary castors. She wanted that bed quite fiercely when she thought about it. But she did not think that as a new girl she could choose it.

'Any you like. Most would choose the window one. I would myself.'

'Oh, so would I,' Charlotte cried. 'Can I really have that one?'

'You're here first, aren't you?' asked Sarah.

It was odd then that Sarah remained, staring out of the window, swinging the window cord, remote-seeming and separate. But Charlotte had an impression suddenly that Sarah had something to say to her. Once she turned round and opened her mouth to speak, but looked back to the window again before any words were formed. Charlotte stood behind her awkwardly and did not know whether to remain there or move away.

Beyond the bedroom door, down the long linoleum-covered passages she heard feet begin to thud and scurry and voices begin to call, the sound both channelled and enlarged by the passages as if they were sounding-boards, until the whole building seemed to buzz and hum. Sarah turned more urgently and started to speak, but at that moment several pairs of feet thumped down the steps outside, skidded on the linoleum at the bottom and the door burst open. Four girls jostled in the doorway.

'Hullo, Elizabeth, Janet, Vanessa,' said Sarah, friendly but quite detached.

'Hullo, Sarah,' the three said, polite but less friendly, Charlotte thought. The fourth girl had dark curly hair and looked rather red about the eyes as if she had been crying; she giggled now for no reason, showing unexpectedly white teeth.

'I'm Susannah,' she said eagerly. 'I'm a new girl, you know.'

'This is Charlotte who is also new. You can keep each other company. Oh, since Charlotte was here first I told her she had first choice of beds. She chose the window bed.'

Sarah did not look at Charlotte again, but smiled briefly, generally, and went out.

For a moment Charlotte was stared at in silence. Susannah and Elizabeth began to smile at her. But Vanessa said sharply, 'Trust snooty Sarah to let the new girl take the best bed.'

'I don't mind which bed *I* have, honestly,' Susannah cried.

'Nor do I.' Charlotte blushed unhappily, grabbing her case off the bed on which she had set it again. 'I don't mind having another bed.'

But she did mind, ridiculously.

'Oh, you'd better keep it now.' Vanessa was grudging if perhaps less sharp. Her freckled nose was pointed, her straight hair pale as paper. 'You'd better keep it if snooty Sarah said. She thinks she's queen of the school that's all, just because her sisters were here, and her mother donkey's years ago.'

'Still it's not Charlotte's fault,' added Janet more kindly.

'How did you get here first anyway?' Vanessa asked. 'Why didn't you have to report to the staffroom, like us?'

'Sarah said she'd do it for me, since I was new.'

'Goodness, isn't she kind to you? Getting you the best bed too. Do you know her at home or something?'

'No . . .' Charlotte was puzzled, for Sarah's kindness did seem odd. 'I don't know her. I don't know anyone here at all.'

By supper time though Charlotte knew all about Susannah, about her family, her father and mother and brother and sister (they were all just like Susannah, judging by their photographs), about her cats and dogs and ponies and guinea pigs, about the time she had been bridesmaid and the time she had broken her leg and the time she had been to France. She had been shown each of the photographs and ornaments which decorated Susannah's chest-of-drawers and envied them a little, having brought none herself so that her own chest-of-drawers remained bare and impersonal. After a while, Susannah's family seemed more real to Charlotte than the school yet seemed. She scarcely felt as real herself, indeed spent much of her time hunting for her name; on lists: games lists, table lists, class lists, cloakroom lists; on everything, everywhere: lockers, pegs, drawers, clothes, shoes, even on her toothbrush and sponge, as if she needed it to prove her own reality. When she was not looking she was writing her name, and not just *Charlotte* either as she would have put on her books at home, or even at the little village school where she went before. *Charlotte* alone proved no identity at all. *Charlotte Mary Makepeace* she wrote in full and in her best handwriting on each of the differently coloured exercise books given to her. Besides the satisfaction she found in writing so carefully it seemed comforting also to prove so emphatically over and over again that she was still Charlotte Makepeace just as she had been yesterday at home. For since this morning she had felt herself to be so many different people and half of them she did not recognize.

Next morning Charlotte woke before the bell. At least no bell had woken her and she doubted if she would have slept through it on only the second day of term. As she floated out of sleep she remembered it was Sunday so that the bell would be rung quite late in any case.

She lay with her eyes shut for a while, comfortable as a cat, the sun warm and rosy on her lids. When at last she opened them she found she was looking almost into the sun itself, though its dazzle was broken by a tree. In return it blurred the dark limits of the tree's branches, beamed through them in places and shone full into her eyes, making her blink.

The tree; Charlotte sat up with a jump. For there should be no tree in the sun's way. In fact you would not expect to see the sun at all because the new building should have hidden it.

But though there had been a building there yesterday and no tree, today there was a tree and no building. The tree was a huge, dark cedar tree.

# CHAPTER TWO

CHARLOTTE shot back down the bed, hiding her head beneath the covers. It must be a dream. If she counted ten before looking out again she would find she had imagined it. As a little girl she'd often lain like that under the bedclothes, counting, but hoping to open her eyes on a different world – a palace perhaps, herself a princess – whereas now she merely wanted things the same as yesterday, the red brick building, the shadowed room; no sun, no tree. Having counted to a hundred just to make sure, she peered out again to find the sun still there with its coloured, dusty beams; also the cedar tree.

Slowly, reluctantly, she turned her head to look into the room itself. Her sun-dazzled eyes could tell scarcely more at first than its shape and colour, both still apparently the same. She could see black iron bedsteads too, four of them, but as her sight cleared saw that against the wall opposite where the fifth bed should have been, was a huge white-painted cupboard with drawers underneath. All the proper chests-of-drawers had gone, and their photographs and ornaments, their dogs and cats and gnomes, their calendars and combs and hairbrushes; so had the curtained cubicle and the washbasin with its shining taps. In place of that a white enamel basin stood on a stand, a white enamel jug inside it. On the chair beside Charlotte's bed instead of her new book there lay a little prayer book in a floppy leather cover and a rather shabby Bible with gold-edged pages.

Janet and Vanessa must have got up early, Charlotte thought wildly, for two of the beds were empty, their coverings smooth as if not slept in at all. They must have made their beds and gone out so quietly that no one had woken.

But that did not explain why the cupboard stood where Elizabeth's bed should have been, nor why the hair on Susannah's pillow next to her own was no longer dark like Susannah's hair, but a lightish brown.

The hump beneath the blankets stirred. There was a little groaning and sighing and a hand reached out, curling itself and uncurling again, terrifying Charlotte, because if she did not know who the hand belonged to and the light brown hair, how would that person know who Charlotte was, and however was she to explain her presence there?

The hump spoke. 'Clare,' it said crossly. '*Clare.*'

Charlotte looked wildly about, but found no one to answer, except herself.

'*Clare*, are you awake?' demanded the hump, more crossly than ever.

'I'm awake,' Charlotte said, which was true, without her having to admit she was not Clare, whoever Clare might be.

'Well then, why didn't you say so before?'

'I . . .' began Charlotte. 'Because I . . .' And then to her horror the girl in the other bed sat up abruptly. She was quite a little girl, much smaller than Susannah, indeed she looked smaller than anyone Charlotte had seen so far at boarding school, though she wore the regulation nightdress. She had long hair and a round face, puzzled rather than cross and red and creased looking on the side nearest Charlotte on which she must have been lying.

She looked at Charlotte as if she saw just whom she expected to see and said, 'Is it early, Clare? Has the bell gone? Have we got to get up?'

'But I'm not Clare,' Charlotte began to say hopelessly, then stopped herself, explanation being impossible, especially since this girl seemed to think so incredibly that she was Clare.

'What's the matter with you, Clare?' the little girl cried. 'Why don't you answer me? Is it time to get up? Is it, is it, *is* it?'

'I haven't heard a bell yet,' Charlotte said.

'Oh, well, then it can't be time to get up. We mustn't be late. Aunt Dolly said we'd get into fearful trouble if we were late for breakfast at school.'

Charlotte was scarcely listening, thinking, horrified, that perhaps she was not Charlotte any more but had changed into someone else. That would explain why the little girl had greeted her as Clare.

She held out her hands to see. They did not look any different, but she wondered suddenly if she knew them well enough to tell. They were quite ordinary hands, having fingers of medium length and no scars or marks to distinguish them. With her hands she stroked her hair, which was quite straight and fell some way below her shoulders just as it had done the day before. When she picked up a piece and drew it round, it seemed the same colour too, fairish, nondescript. She moved her hands rapidly over all her face, eyes, mouth, chin, cheeks, nose, and then again, more slowly. But it did not tell her very much. Could you just by feel, she wondered, recognize your own face? A blind person might, whose touch was sight, but she was not sure she could trust herself to do it. Her mouth seemed wider than she'd thought, her nose felt narrower.

'What are you feeling your face for like that?' the little girl was asking curiously.

'Oh . . . oh . . . nothing in particular . . .' And at that moment, luckily, the bell went, an old-fashioned clanging bell, not the shrill electric one of the night before. Charlotte jumped out of bed immediately, but the other huddled back into hers, saying, 'I don't feel a bit like getting up, but of course you do what we ought, Clare, you always do.'

Charlotte was by now so desperate she did not care if the girl found her odd. She ran to the only mirror in the room, a square, rather stained and pitted one hung just beside the door, and the relief that came when she saw her own face staring back at her was huger than she could have thought.

Except, if she was Charlotte, why did the little girl take her for somebody else called Clare? Just then the door opened and a woman came in, a tall, thin woman with her hair screwed up on her head under a white cap like a nurse's cap, her head very small like the knob on a knitting needle. Her big white apron was starched to shine, indeed she shone all over as if newly polished: shoes, hair, apron, even her nose. Her skirt, Charlotte noticed, was so long it stopped not far above her ankles.

'Emily? Isn't it?' she said to Charlotte. 'Are you so vain, Emily, that you must stare at yourself before breakfast.'

Charlotte looked at her quite speechlessly, but Emily shot up in bed and said indignantly, 'She's not Emily, she's Clare, *I'm* Emily.'

'I do beg your pardon, then, Emily,' said the woman, sarcastically. 'Just to remind you *I* am Nurse Gregory. Did you not hear the bell, Emily? Get out of your bed at once. Just because you sleep here as a convenience . . .' (And what does that mean? thought Charlotte) – 'just because you sleep here as a convenience does not mean you may take liberties or disregard the rules.'

'Oh, I don't think she meant to. I don't think she knew you had to get up at once.' Charlotte found herself automatically defending Emily, just as she had always defended her own sister Emma, at home.

'But it's a whole half-hour to breakfast,' Emily was protesting on her own behalf. 'It doesn't take me half an hour to get dressed.' The nurse looked from her to Charlotte with a smile that had glitter but no friendliness.

'Do I take it then you are a dirty little girl and never properly wash yourself?'

'I wash very well indeed,' cried Emily indignantly. 'Don't I, Clare? Our Aunt Dolly says I wash very well . . .'

'Does she not also tell you, Emily, that it is rude to answer back? I shall return in fifteen minutes and expect to find you both ready, save your hair, which I shall plait myself today.'

'Clare always plaits my hair for me.'

'No doubt,' said Nurse Gregory, turning to the door. 'But I shall do it for today.'

If Emily was rebellious Charlotte was relieved at this, never having plaited hair before. She was also (foolishly she thought and irrelevantly) quite pleased at the idea of having her hair in plaits, which she had always wanted secretly and never been allowed, because her grandfather with whom she lived did not like girls to have their hair in plaits. Besides to think foolish, irrelevant thoughts was more comfortable than fighting her way through the impossible ones; what was happening to her, and why and how.

The uniform she had to wear was not unlike the one she had worn yesterday, if less well-fitting. Under it, despite the sun, went a thick woollen vest and bodice, thick navy-blue knickers and thick black stockings. Charlotte had not worn stockings the day before.

All the while she dressed herself and helped Emily do up her buttons, all the while Nurse Gregory was coming and plaiting their hair – using the comb more as if to dissect heads – and while afterwards she and Emily knelt on the chilly linoleum to say their prayers, Charlotte was trying in her mind to describe how things seemed to her that morning; the room, Nurse Gregory, the clothes she wore. There was some particular word she wanted. She could not, in these confusions, think what it was. Nurse Gregory had pulled her hair so tightly into its single plait, tied ribbon so tightly at top and bottom, that her scalp ached and pricked still, which made her brain seem to ache and prickle too. The more she hunted for this word, the more confused she felt.

Outside the room was the same – or it looked the same – a horde of blue-clad girls whose faces she did not know, the same thud of feet and clatter of voices, the same mazed passages and stairs as yesterday, except that she thought (or had she dreamed it?) that the walls had been white then, while today they were brown. Yesterday they had eaten in a large white-wall room where today they ate in an oak panelled one, beneath a picture of a man with eyes black as buttons and a stiff white clergyman's collar. She thought she recognized the picture though she did not recognize the room. The trouble was that she had found everything so strange and confusing yesterday in a new school that now, even when she shut her eyes and tried to remember, she could not really tell what had changed about her and what had not. She began to wonder whether perhaps she had dreamed before or even was dreaming today.

The porridge for breakfast was brought round by maids in uniform. There had been no maids yesterday Charlotte was sure. The uniforms were black and white and looked she thought as Nurse Gregory had – and again she fumbled for the right word, but this time it swam into her head quite easily – they looked old-fashioned. Their skirts were rather too long for one thing like Nurse Gregory's. Of course she thought, some people just did wear longish skirts and old-fashioned clothes, Miss Gozzling for example, her grandfather's housekeeper. Old-fashioned was the word she wanted anyway, the one her mind had chased so uselessly before. Everything this morning did seem old-fashioned; in obvious ways, such as there being no washbasin, no electric bell, and in other less obvious ways than that. But then her home Aviary Hall was just as old-fashioned, if not more so, having been decorated and furnished many years ago and scarcely altered since. No doubt this school was the same she told herself firmly, for a different explanation that slid into her mind was, though simple, so huge and impossible that she could not believe it, did not even want to. It frightened her. She turned her mind wildly away, thinking how funny – I haven't heard any aeroplanes this morning. I wonder why.

As they filed into the brown-panelled dining room each girl had taken from a scrubbed shelf a small glass jar containing a slab of margarine, like butter in texture, but very much paler in colour. Fortunately Emily had fetched Charlotte's as well as her own, for on each was stuck a little white label with a name on it, and Charlotte would not have known which name to take. *E. Moby*, Emily's label said, *C. Moby*, Charlotte's. Everyone placed their jars on the table in front of them and so therefore did Charlotte and Emily.

'Wake up, dreamy,' a voice prodded at Charlotte from the other side of the table; a surprisingly deep imposing voice, for it belonged to a small round girl with spectacles and with black hair cut quite short instead of long in a plait like most people's. She had also a very snub nose. Just now she was contorting herself to read the name on Charlotte's jar.

'Wake up, dreamy. What's the C stand for?'

'C?' asked Charlotte, jerked out of thought. 'What do you mean C?'

'On your marge jar, silly. C. Moby it says. I'm asking you your name in other words . . .'

'Oh . . . Char . . .' began Charlotte, off guard still, but Emily took over answering before the name was fully out.

'She's Clare. I'm Emily. What's the M on yours?'

'Marjorie, if you must know, but everyone calls me Bunty, Marjorie's an awful name. You can call me Bunty too, if you like. Do you want sugar on your porridge or milk?'

'Both, of course,' said Emily.

'You can't have both, because of the war. You have to choose. What I wanted to tell you was that I'd have sugar if I were you, it's horrid otherwise. It's pretty horrid with sugar too, actually, my sister's a landgirl now and she says what they give pigs on her farm is better than school porridge.'

'Sssh, Bunty, you mustn't talk like that, you'll get into awful trouble if someone hears,' whispered her neighbour, a thin droopy girl with brown eyes like butter drops and sandy-coloured hair and lashes.

'Oh, don't be such a prig, Ruth,' Bunty said impatiently. 'Did you come late yesterday?' she asked Emily, her mouth already full of porridge. 'I didn't see you at supper.'

'We were quite late,' said Emily. 'In time for supper though.'

'Well, I never saw you. Are you two sisters?'

'Clare's my brother if you must know.'

'There's no need to be cheeky, you're just a little new girl, remember. You don't much look like sisters, that's all.'

'How long have you been here then?' asked Emily.

'One term. That's nearly five months, including the holidays.'

'One term? *One* term? Well, that's nothing to be so grand about.'

There was a pause. Bunty turned her back on Emily as far as it was possible and ate her porridge. Charlotte hoped that she would not remain offended for long. She hoped Bunty would ask a great many more questions, for she was not in a position to ask them for herself, much as she wanted to. At last Bunty leaned across the table in a lordly way.

'How old is Emily? She looks rather a baby to be at boarding school?'

'I'm *not a baby*,' Emily cried indignantly. 'I was ten in August.'

'Ten, just ten. You are a baby then, just as I thought. I didn't know anyone could come here till they were eleven.'

'How old are you then?'

'I'm eleven actually.'

'Well, there's nothing to be so grand about. Clare's thirteen.'

'Thirteen! Gosh, she doesn't look as ancient as that. But what are you doing here if you're only ten?'

'We hadn't anywhere else to go if you must know.'

'Everything's upside-down with the war of course,' observed Bunty in an elderly voice.

'But it wasn't the war at all, it was our Aunt Dolly. She was ill you see, and we live with her in term-time.'

'Did you go to a day-school before then?'

'We've been to lots and lots of schools. As a matter of fact,' said Emily impressively, 'this is my fifth school.'

'Your fifth school? Gosh, how *ripping*, you lucky thing. I've only been to one. I had a governess before.'

Charlotte meanwhile struggled through her porridge, which was as solid as bread, much solider in lumps, and slippery too. Emily pushed hers away after one mouthful. Bunty told her she'd have to eat it, that was the rule, but the maid who came to clear smiled and shrugged and took pity on her, removing the plate quickly before the teacher at the end of the table had noticed anything.

'Miss Bite says it's doing your bit, to eat things you don't like,' Bunty said. 'I don't see how it hurts Germans myself, eating nasty porridge.'

'I couldn't have eaten it if it made us win the war,' said Emily passionately.

'Well, I'm so hungry I could eat anything. Bags your second round of bread, Emily, if you don't want it, we're only allowed two each you see, and that still leaves me starving.'

'Oh, but I will want it. I have to eat something.'

'You can have mine, Bunty,' Charlotte said.

'You are a sport, Clare, thanks awfully. Can I have some of your marge ration too, mine will never last otherwise.'

But even having eaten very fast three slices of bread with her own and some of Charlotte's margarine, Bunty still watched every bite Emily took, like, Charlotte thought, a hungry little dog.

Except for the mysterious, and to Charlotte incomprehensible talk about the war – *what* war could Bunty mean? – everything seemed so ordinary that she thought there must be some quite simple explanation for what had happened to her. She could begin to believe this was just a different school, its likeness with yesterday's merely the likeness of any boarding school to any other. This at least was what she wanted to believe.

But then after breakfast she went upstairs and except for the cedar tree the view out of the window was unmistakably the same view as yesterday, of garden and river and island. Nor could she mistake her bed with its wheels like little wagon-wheels. And when later she set out for the church in the school crocodile, it was from the same porticoed door at which the bus had arrived yesterday, though beyond, inexplicably, all the lawns that had been green yesterday were not lawns any more but dug up and planted with cabbages.

Charlotte and Emily wore gloves and carried prayer books as did everyone. They were meant to keep silence on their way. 'It's so that we can think holy thoughts for church you see,' Bunty explained. 'Not that I ever seem to have any.'

'Oh, Clare's always thinking holy thoughts, aren't you, Clare?' Emily replied, with a meaningful glance at Charlotte that Charlotte quite missed the meaning of since she was not Clare, nor knew her.

Through the school gates they marched – to these now fixed a pair of Union Jacks, very faded, as if they had been there some considerable time and in all kinds of weathers. The road beyond was more countrified than Charlotte had thought it yesterday. She could not remember seeing market gardens behind high walls, their rows of green houses flashing in the sun like a field of huge glass furrows.

# CHAPTER THREE

NEXT morning when Charlotte awoke to an aeroplane's booming overhead and saw Susannah asleep next to her, she at once thought Emily merely a dream; what had happened impossible unless a dream. For she had behaved so calmly and ordinarily; had even written a Sunday letter home to Emily's Aunt Dolly whom she had never seen, and by the evening had accepted the day almost as any other day, not one out of her own time at all. Now she assumed she had gone to sleep on Saturday night, dreamed a most vivid dream about Sunday from which she had woken at last to find the real Sunday ahead of her.

But the rising bell went not long afterwards, the one-note, electric bell, at seven o'clock, weekday time. The others grumbled their way out of bed into weekday shirts and tunics, not Sunday coats and skirts.

'Gosh, Monday mornings. How I hate Monday mornings,' Vanessa sighed. But if it was Monday it meant Charlotte had missed out a whole day in her own time. It meant Emily was no dream but real.

Yesterday she thought she must have been quite numbed by the strangeness to have behaved as she did, so normally, though in another time, and in wartime too. Today, contrariwise, she was overcome by it, stopping, thinking, trembling every now and then.

She did not know when exactly she had realized what had happened to her. Not knowing had slid so gradually into half guessing, half knowing, knowing for certain. She thought herself stupid now for not realizing immediately, as children did in books; but of course they usually went back so much further into the past when it was easier to tell because people dressed, unmistakably, in wigs or crinolines.

Then, at bedtime yesterday she had found beneath Clare's Bible on the chair a thin red exercise book. *Diary*, it had said on the cover, and *Clare Mary Moby*; and beneath that again in

letters three times larger, *PRIVATE*. Charlotte
had hesitated briefly, holding it in her hands. But
she had been comforted in some odd way because
Clare shared her middle name and even her initials
and at last she had opened it determinedly, though
she was careful still to look only at the date of the
last entry. The day before in her own time, the
present, had been Saturday, 14th September. But
Clare had written, *Saturday, 14th September
1918*, the same day, only over forty years before.

It seemed quite unbelievable now. After breakfast,
her bed half made, Charlotte picked up her
nightdress and stood, far away, letting it dangle
from her hands. She was looking out of the
window at the new brick building which stood
where the cedar tree used to stand. The tree had
been as beautiful as a sailing ship, its trunk stouter
than a mast, its branches spread like sails, and she
felt sad, even indignant that they should have
thought to cut it down. Yet it seemed silly to feel
sad for something lost so long ago, that she ought
never to have seen.

'Penny for them.' Charlotte returned from her
thinking to find Vanessa staring at her, curiously.

'You might have been on Mars, the way you
looked. Penny for your thoughts.'

'Oh. Oh, I see. Nothing very much really.'

'But you must think about something. All yesterday and this morning too, it's been hard to get a word out of you. You must think about something all that time.'

'Oh, Charlotte's just dreamy, aren't you, Charlotte?' Susannah apologized for her.

'Why should she want to talk to us, anyway?' asked Elizabeth, lazily, looking up from her book. 'Lucky Charlotte. Perhaps she can dream herself right out of here.'

Elizabeth was not a thin girl like Janet and Vanessa, not plump exactly either, but big. Her hair, though short, was rough even when brushed and wild when not, as now. She had a big untidy-looking mouth, big untidy-looking hands with the nails chewed down, even untidy-looking skin that was pale and peeled in places. As soon as they had returned from breakfast she flung herself down to read on her unmade bed. A trail of clothes lay on the floor round her and her transistor radio blurted out 'Housewives' Choice'.

Vanessa looked distastefully at Elizabeth.

'Well, we all know you're always too busy reading to hear anything we say, but we can't dream away your mess unfortunately.'

'It's five minutes to the bell, Elizabeth,' said Janet but more patiently. 'Don't you think you'd better get a move on?'

'Gosh, is it really? I'll be *late*,' cried Elizabeth, hurling her nightdress to the floor and rushing out of the room, leaving Janet and Vanessa to make faces at each other and murmur what a mess she was – how they couldn't bear to share a room with her for a whole term.

'She's supposed to be brainy, that's her trouble. She thinks she can get away with anything because of it.' Vanessa turned off the radio. But Elizabeth switched it on again, quite casually, when she returned.

From all the confusion Charlotte's mind groped out one thing – that no one had missed her yesterday. But it was not until later that the obvious explanation struck home to her. That while she herself had taken Clare's place yesterday, Clare must have taken hers.

In the library that morning she saw a book called *Twentieth Century Europe*, and when the bell had rung and the rest of the class were collecting their books she lifted it down, hastily, guiltily. She opened it at the back, leafing through till she came to the chapters on the Second World War. Earlier yesterday she had thought that might be the war then being fought, but now she saw it had started in 1939. At once she slammed the book firmly shut. She did not want to check further the dates of the other, the First World War. She did not want to read of it at all. It seemed like cheating somehow, like looking at the end of a book before you were halfway through. It even seemed unlucky. Of course she might never go back into 1918. Yet in an odd and melancholy way she hoped she might. She did not want to do anything that might prevent it, even something so simple as checking on a date.

The very next morning when she woke beside Emily again, Charlotte, pleased, gave her a special smile of greeting; before being reminded by her look of surprise, that as far as Emily was concerned she had been there all the time.

Emily was silent today. From time to time she looked most oddly at Charlotte, who wondered uncomfortably if she was beginning to guess that something strange was happening.

'I say,' Bunty said when they went to their classroom after prayers, 'I say, I wanted to ask you. If you're thirteen, aren't you a bit old to be in a class with me and Emily?'

'It's just because we've been to so many schools, she's never had a chance to catch up,' cried Emily fiercely. 'Clare's very clever, really she is, so snubs to you and utterly squash.'

'I never said she was stupid, did I, stupid? Anyway, can't she ever answer for herself?'

'And can't you ever stop asking questions? Someone of thirteen can't be bothered with all your silly questions, that's all.'

'Was there ever such a cheeky little new bug as you?' asked Bunty, amiably.

Their classroom was a big room with two pillars at one end above the dais where the teacher sat, surveying both their class and another one. In Charlotte's time this was used as a dining-hall, while her class lived in a little cell-like place at the end of the new glass-covered way that ran along beside a stable yard. The classroom there might once have been the saddle-room, with its three high windows and stone walls, with the three stone steps that led to a door kept permanently locked. It was very small, very dark compared to this large, light, dusty room. The clicking of the rings on the green baize curtains covering the pigeon holes sounded the same in both the classrooms, however.

Charlotte went upstairs at break to fetch a handkerchief, up the steep back stairs that emerged by the window overlooking the yard. The window was open and there was nobody in sight. Hastily, guiltily, she thrust out her head and found that with some awkward craning she could see where the classroom should have been. No covered way ran to it now. Its door was painted blue like the other doors in the yard, but the paint was so flaked and old she could see the wood in places underneath; also there was a large padlock on it.

Beneath Charlotte a door opened and a maid came out of the kitchen. Charlotte could see the parting in her hair and smell the steaming reek of food. She brought her head in again hastily to find Nurse Gregory standing behind her, Nurse Gregory's eyes screwing themselves into her.

'And what do you find so interesting then, Clare?' she enquired with interest.

'I – I've just come up to fetch a handkerchief from my room.'

'Handkerchief I suppose growing outside like Virginia creeper?'

Charlotte said no and then yes, meekly, and confusedly since an answer seemed expected, but either way convicted her, yes, of stupidity, no, probably of crime, that is of breaking a school rule.

'The rule is, no girl may come up to her bedroom during the day. You should have remembered your handkerchief this morning.'

'But I thought,' said Charlotte, 'honestly, I thought the rules said . . .' And then she remembered she had heard the rules read in her own time, not here, and that there weren't necessarily the same rules now. But she could not use this for an excuse. 'I didn't know the rules,' she ended lamely, pulling down the rather short tunic they wore on weekdays in 1918, not unlike the modern one except for the strip of velvet across its top.

'That is no excuse. You should have known. I read them to you myself only yesterday. It is not, of course, a rule you'll long be in a position to break, since you will be in lodgings soon and come only as a day-girl here.'

'Lodgings?' asked Charlotte, amazed, but Nurse Gregory noticed no amazement, her voice clattering on as if it were set by clockwork and had to go running down.

'I cannot spare my sickroom long, you know. I have two girls ill already in the other one and if there are more I shall soon need your room. I hope you and Emily quite realize the kindness Miss Bite did you in allowing you its use till lodgings could be found. Were it not for wartime, such sudden upsets and arrangements could never be allowed.'

'Everything's upside-down with the war,' ventured Charlotte, remembering what Bunty had said.

'I am not upside-down and my order-mark system works perfectly. You will take one please and go straight downstairs again.'

All the rest of that morning Charlotte had to do what she usually told her sister not to do; wipe her nose on the back of her hand. She was wondering too, what would happen once the Mobys went into lodgings and did not sleep at school. Would she and Clare continue to change about? And suppose she should get stuck here, could not get back to her proper time to be Charlotte instead of Clare, to have Emma for her sister instead of Emily? The thought of that frightened her and she tried hard not to think about it.

## CHAPTER FOUR

THERE was work to be prepared that day for future lessons. This did not create such difficulty as it might have done. Charlotte's handwriting was not unlike Clare's, since she had been taught to form her letters in the same old-fashioned way as Clare formed hers. Also the system of work had not changed much between present and past. Charlotte, being organized and neat, followed it as meticulously as Clare had done, jotting down in the little notebooks provided not only the work to be done but the date by which it had to be handed in. They had been set an essay called *My Holidays* and she was thankful to find that it could be left till another day, for how could she write an essay about Clare's holidays? She knew nothing about them, nor had she any means of finding out. And if she did write something and Emily read it, how suspicious she would be, if she was not suspicious already, as Charlotte had begun to think. She did arithmetic instead, long division of money that she had learnt when much younger and so found easy, although she was not usually good at arithmetic. She also learnt by heart the six verses of a poem called *How Horatius Kept the Bridge:*

> *Lars Porsena of Clusium*
> *By the Nine Gods he swore*
> *That the great house of Tarquin*
> *Should suffer wrong no more.*

It was stirring both to learn and to recite and kept on beating in Charlotte's head all that day and the next, in her own time.

That morning when Charlotte awoke she had found beside her bed an exercise book with a pale pink cover (the colour usually used for scripture books) on which was written *Charlotte Mary Makepeace* and underneath again blacked over twice, *VERY PRIVATE.* Charlotte hesitated before opening this. There was something disconcerting about a book which had her own name on it, that no one ought to have written except herself, and yet which she had not written. Nor was her name now her property alone. Suppose that *VERY PRIVATE* warned her not to open the book and read what was inside?

However, she opened the book at last, to read not unexpectedly but still as disconcertingly a message from someone whom she did not know and who was more than forty years away from her.

*Dear Charlotte,* she read. *I think we should be able to write to each other to explain anything difficult. For instance, about work and about Emily. (Please look after Emily. She's only ten.) We could use this book here and my diary in 1918, it is that red book on the chair. But please do not read the earlier part. It is very private. Not even Emily may read it. I did your arithmetic for you today. I am afraid it was all wrong. I am so bad at arithmetic.*

*Please write. I think it would help if we both write. Yours sincerely, Clare. P. S. I took this book from the classroom cupboard. It was very dishonest and wrong of me, but I could not think what else to do.*

Clare's arithmetic certainly was not good. Charlotte had that book back that day, scored in red ink, with only two marks given out of ten, and decided that in future she had better try to do it for herself. She was going to suggest this to Clare that very evening in her own note, but it seemed rather unkind and so after all she left it out.

*Dear Clare,* she wrote: *It was very clever of you to think of this book. I don't think it was too wrong to take it from the cupboard. We have to have a book and there's no other way of finding one. I think grown-ups would say it was all right if they knew what was happening to us. I promise not to read your diary. I did open it once just to find out the date, but I promise on my honour I didn't read any more. I promise. By the way, do you think we should tell Emily what's happening? I'm sure she's suspicious, so it might be better. But I think you should tell her, perhaps, not me.* Charlotte stopped and thought a little and then added: *How are you managing here? Do you find it very difficult and strange?*

For it had occurred to her suddenly how much harder it must be to move forward in time than to move back. At least in the past many things were familiar, and you knew something about it. But what did you know about the future? – nothing, except guesses and many of them frightening. She would not have liked to move forty or fifty years ahead of her own time, as Clare had moved ahead of hers.

Susannah was saying curiously, 'Whatever do you find to write about? I kept a diary once and all I could think of to say was, had breakfast, had lunch, had tea, and went to bed.'

'Oh, I just think of things,' said Charlotte, ending her letter hastily.

*I don't think anything important happened today. I'll write tomorrow. Yours sincerely, Charlotte. P. S. I can't understand why this is happening, can you? P. P. S. I didn't look at your diary, honestly.*

Afterwards out of the darkness a voice came, Vanessa's voice. 'Charlotte, are you awake?'

'Yes, of course.'

'Janet and I are very puzzled. Why do you take such ages to say your prayers some nights before you get into bed, and not other nights at all.'

'Well, some nights I say them in bed,' Charlotte answered, glad of the dark. From now on she thought she would have to do as Clare did and kneel beside her bed, much as she would hate to make such display of holiness, otherwise the rest of them might become suspicious. It was odd really that they were not suspicious already.

Charlotte lay awake some while that night. She could hear the sounds of traffic in the distance, blown down-river from the new road bridge, and occasionally the sounds of trains too, from the railway bridge.

When the aeroplanes came they blotted out all the other sounds. She thought how frightening they must have seemed to Clare at first. Whatever had she thought such enormous sounds could be? The school itself was not so very different from the earlier one, but in 1918 so far Charlotte had only heard one aeroplane and that a tiny buzzing far away, which had quite excited Emily, who cried, 'A plane, a plane! Can you see it, Bunty? Can you see it, Clare?'

These airliners did not buzz, unless it was inside your head like something drilling there. Some roared, some screamed, some thundered, some did all three at once. Some made tight narrow sounds, loud yet contained within a space, others laid sound flat over your head like a kind of roof; still others, and by far the worst, were heavy, they reverberated everywhere as though the air made little invisible walls against which sound echoed, through which it broke in thunderous waves and surgings; until it felt like being in a tent of sound pegged close all round. Then sometimes Charlotte found it hard to remember who she was, Charlotte, or Clare, or someone quite different again.

It was odd, disconcerting, this jerky proceeding of days in worlds both so different, and yet in the movements of school alike – for they continued to change about day after day. The earlier school was stricter, it was true, more drab, the food there both scarcer and nastier. They had fur in the soup on Tuesday, underboiled fish on Wednesday, and on Thursday the most unpleasant pudding Charlotte had ever eaten – North Pole pudding, it was called – a kind of jelly made of cornmeal, grey like porridge, shiny like glue and flecked with little pieces of meal like the flaws in glass. Emily would not eat it and was made to sit in the dining room for hours. But she smuggled the plateful into her handkerchief when no one was looking and reappeared in class triumphantly.

Between Emily and Susannah and the rest, Charlotte felt as if she were reading two stories alternately, reaching some point of tension in one, only to continue in the other. It was Friday, for instance, before she received an answer to her first note to Clare, which said, among other things:

> *I don't think we should tell Emily. I don't want to tell her because I think she might be frightened and not understand. Please, Charlotte, just go on acting as if you were me, and not say anything and look after her.*

But of course Charlotte could not look after Emily that day because it was her own time and there was no Emily. There were Janet and Vanessa instead, who seemed to be plotting something and giggled a great deal. After supper they said to Charlotte and Susannah, 'Don't come up just yet. One of us will fetch you when we're ready.'

Charlotte went on ahead when the time came and opened the door to find the curtains drawn, the light masked with a sweater. A figure leapt out at her from the gloom – Vanessa – while Janet grabbed Susannah from behind. Susannah let out a giggle, a little sharp nervous 'Oh . . .'

'Now,' they were told by deep, croaking, cracking voices, 'now, o novices, you have tests to undergo. Lie down and look up these.'

'These' were dressing-gown sleeves and trembled rather because Janet and Vanessa who held them were laughing so much. Only Elizabeth took no part. She lay on her bed with her back to everyone, reading by the light of a torch, and Charlotte heard her radio faintly, indecipherably, growl. She was waiting, apprehensive, for something to happen, staring up through the tunnel of the dressing-gown sleeve. It was Janet's dressing gown, very thick and hairy, tickling her mouth and nose, making her want to sneeze. She could see an uneven round of light at the top of it, but this was suddenly obscured, by what she could not tell.

'Behold the sights of Venice,' intoned Vanessa's voice above Charlotte and Janet's above Susannah. Charlotte screwed up her eyes to see, but still could not make nothing out at all. The round of light appeared again and was more obscured.

'Behold the churches of Venice,' they said. And afterwards again: 'Behold the bridges of Venice.'

There was a long pause. The voices began at last more loudly and impressively than ever: 'Behold the canals of Venice'; but were overcome by giggles well before the end, for down the dressing-gown sleeves came a cascade of icy water on to the faces of Charlotte and Susannah, who sat up choking, startled, bewildered, rubbing the water from their eyes and mouths while Janet and Vanessa collapsed with laughing, clutched each other and laughed the more.

'What did you do that for?' cried Susannah indignantly. 'I'm all wet. You made me wet.'

'You made me wet,' they mimicked. 'That's the point, silly. That's the joke, it's a joke you see.'

'Well, I don't think it's awfully funny that sort of thing, making people wet.' Susannah was in tears by now.

'As if you can make wet people wetter anyway,' they cried. 'All new girls have this done. You'll be able to do it on someone else next term. It's very funny really and we haven't finished yet. They're sort of initiation tests.'

Before they could start another test, however, there was a knock on the door and a prefect came in with a message for Susannah. Seeing the mess of water she grew shocked and stern and made them clear it up at once. She made them pull the sweater from the light and draw the curtains back.

The prefect happened to be Sarah. Charlotte had not spoken to her since the first day of term, and she was cold and distant now, though she did smile once in Charlotte's direction:

When she had gone Susannah cried and Elizabeth started to laugh. Vanessa said how feeble they all were not to take a joke, what rotten luck it was for her and Janet to be landed with such a wet lot as this. When the same trick had been played on them, they had not minded, of course they hadn't. They weren't such spoilsports. Tricks like that had been played on new girls for absolutely donkey's years, since before Sarah's mother came, she wouldn't wonder.

Elizabeth stopped laughing at her after a little and became argumentative, waving her hands about to enforce her point.

'Why don't you grow up, you two, for goodness' sake? Some people hate having water thrown in their face, and I don't blame them one little bit.'

'It's only meant to be a joke, Elizabeth,' protested Janet.

Vanessa said coldly, 'Oh, don't be such a prig. You can't talk anyway. You're a prig and Susannah's a cry baby – and Charlotte – well, Charlotte's just standoffish. She never says a word or talks to us. What a hopeless lot.'

Charlotte did not much like being called standoffish. But it was so difficult when she was only here every other day. Often she did not know what had happened, what was going on, and she was afraid of showing it, of saying things that might make everyone suspicious. It seemed safer usually not to speak at all.

She wondered about Sarah's mother, whether she had had the tricks played on her; whether they had been played in 1918 too. How long ago had Sarah's mother come to the school? She must be quite old now with all her children grown up except for Sarah.

She began, quite vaguely at first, to add up the dates. But after a while she added more accurately, more carefully, realizing, with a shock that Clare and Emily could be alive still, in the present. In fact they would be much younger than her own grandfather, Elijah. Charlotte was not at all sure she found that thought comfortable. She did not want to meet an elderly Emily while knowing the ten-year-old.

# CHAPTER FIVE

ON Saturday morning Emily ignored Charlotte pointedly, turning her back on her when they had to be together in their bedroom or at their double classroom desk, and then, after lunch, when they set out on the school walk she partnered Bunty, leaving Ruth and Charlotte, both rather disconsolate, to go together.

They went across the river to the great park at the top of the hill. An army training camp lay just inside its gates. Wheels had injured the smooth turf there. Lorries were ranged in the shade of the trees, their bonnets painted tree colour as camouflage, green and brown and grey – indeed everything except the autumn trees was green and brown and grey – the lorries, the huts, the soldiers dressed in khaki who strolled casually about or marched stiffly up and down. One squad was drilling. The sergeant, his moustache as wide as horns, gave indistinguishable bellows, each one so huge it seemed to contain its own echo. The soldiers were like a single block, not individual men. They stopped, wheeled, halted to the bellows, their arms swinging up simultaneously like flaps or shelves.

Bunty pointed to the sergeant and whispered something to Emily, who began to giggle.

'Tenshun!' roared Bunty in her deep impressive voice. Emily put her arm out as if it held a rifle and began to march. The teacher, Miss Wilkin, a plump little woman, like a bird, was far ahead of them, talking to an older girl, and did not turn.

'Tenshun! Left, right. Left, right. Left, right,' shouted Bunty. Left, right, marched Emily, exaggeratedly, giggling.

'Bunty – oh, Bunty, *don't*, please don't,' cried Ruth but hopelessly. For others were imitating Emily now, some self-conscious about it, some not at all, girls called Olive – Peggy – Dorothy – Susan – Joan. They let Bunty drill them, holding themselves upright, sloping imaginary arms, marching stiff as soldiers. More and more joined in. Bunty's orders grew louder, louder. Emily pranced so exaggeratedly she might have been a horse, not a soldier any more.

'Oh, Bunty, stop,' cried Ruth.

'Emily, stop it,' Charlotte said, but Emily glanced at her defiantly and carried on more furiously than ever.

The soldiers near the fence had begun to laugh at them, to shout and point. The noise came to Miss Wilkin's ears at last, and she hurried back, her hair fluffed out, her hat tipped at an angle. She was one of the youngest school teachers; Charlotte had seen her skip upstairs once when she thought no one was watching, as if she were as young as Emily. She wore an engagement ring which she glanced at constantly and touched and turned, but she was not touching or looking at it now.

'Olive, Dorothy, Joan,' she was scolding, scarlet in the face. 'Bunty, whatever are you doing?' Some of the soldiers whistled and winked at her, which did not assist her attempts at dignity.

When the crocodile moved off again, Emily was still giggling. But the grin died as she saw Charlotte's eyes on her and she looked quickly away.

It had grown very hot. All the grass had been rubbed from the track and the earth beneath was cracked and white, its dust soon blurring the shine on polished shoes. Emily began to limp and lag and complain about being too hot. Bunty told her briskly to make less fuss. The trees, though bright, were almost too dry, shabby-looking, the grass was yellow and pale beneath a brilliant sky.

They came to a patch of woodland, oak trees mostly, thickset as old stags, their branches spread like antlers. The children, except for Bunty who was in disgrace, were allowed to wander a little, do as they liked; so Charlotte sat herself down against a tree's gawky roots and rummaged among its debris of leaves and twigs, odd spots of sunlight swinging about her head. She discovered acorns and took them from their cups; but found when she tried to fit one back that it would not fit so well though there seemed no difference in either the acorn or its cup.

She glanced up suddenly to find Emily planted in front of her; rather odd-looking, seen from below, her feet appearing huge, her face elongated, small. She was red with heat, her hat crooked, her mouth and fingers purple with blackberry. She thrust some blackberries down towards Charlotte, and for the first time for days looked at her directly, so making Charlotte blush and turn her face down, away.

'I want you to tell me what's happening,' Emily said angrily. 'Something's happening. You're so odd, not like you at all. As if you were someone different. You've got to tell me. I won't not be told any more. I hate it.'

It would be frightening for Emily, Charlotte thought, quite uncanny and odd. Whatever would she have felt herself to find a stranger in her sister Emma's place, who was nevertheless supposed to be the real Emma? This was really what decided her that Emily must be told; that it would be easier for her to know the truth. She remembered, guiltily, what Clare had said, but Emily had not asked Clare what was happening, as she asked Charlotte now.

She made her voice as gentle and apologetic as she could. 'I'm not Clare. That's why I'm different. Clare's changed places with me. She's me. She'll be back here tomorrow, honestly.'

'Whatever do you mean? How can you not be Clare? Where is she? Where's she gone?' asked Emily wildly.

'It's all right, really, Emily. She's gone into my time instead of me and I've come back into the past, to you.'

'What do you mean? You're crazy. What do you mean – back into the past?' said Emily, disguising panic by truculence so effectively and for such a long time that Charlotte found her patience blanketed after a while and hard to keep. She floundered about in words and sentences, trying to explain it, different ways round, twenty times at least, and each time Emily cried, 'I don't believe it. Things like that don't happen. I don't believe it.'

'All right, don't believe it,' cried Charlotte, made angry at last. It did not help to be so hot, sweating and itching inside her thick school clothes. 'All right, don't believe it. But it's true I tell you.'

'Really really true?' asked Emily, quieter.

'Yes, really true. You can ask Clare tomorrow, if you don't believe me.' Charlotte was ashamed now for being angry and also spoke more calmly. They remained in silence for a little while. There were girls' voices, and squealings, the sound of engines from the army camp. Charlotte found a dried bracken frond on Emily's stocking just by her eyes and crumbled it between her fingers till its brown teeth fell to tiny prickly pieces, not quite to dust on her skin.

Emily squatted down beside her and played with an acorn and its cup. 'What's your name then?' she asked.

'My name?' asked Charlotte.

'If you're not Clare.'

'Charlotte,' said Charlotte.

'Charlotte?' said Emily giggling. 'What a funny old-fashioned name. How funny you've got an old-fashioned name.' And suddenly, she might never have shown disbelief at all. She was not frightened any more, or did not appear to be, not truculent, but excited, pestering Charlotte with questions, insisting on partnering her in the crocodile again and whispering to her about it. Charlotte could even ask questions for herself about things that puzzled her.

'How did you know something was odd. How was I different from Clare?' she asked.

'You were just different. Oh, I don't know.'

'You must know, a *little*.'

'I suppose – well, I suppose, you didn't answer the questions. You didn't – well, you were less bossy, that's all. And . . .'

'That can't be all, it *can't* be.'

'Clare's fearfully holy, sort of, you know, and good, horribly good. You are good in a way, but different.'

'Didn't you guess at all I was really a different person and not just Clare being different?'

'I don't know if I did or not,' said Emily, which was not any answer that Charlotte wanted. For she had approached the question the wrong way round. What she really wanted to know was why Emily had mistaken her for Clare in the first place. Were they so very alike? But she hesitated to ask this, for it was the most baffling and in some ways the most worrying question of all.

Much later, while they were getting ready for bed, Emily said, 'Your bed's different from mine. It's got those funny wheels on it. I wanted it because it was by the window, but Nurse Gregory made Clare have it instead. Do you think it might have something to do with you and Clare changing? Do you think that if I slept there tonight I might end up in your time too?'

'I don't suppose so for a minute,' said Charlotte firmly. It was certainly an interesting, not to say startling idea, but not one she thought to be explored with Emily now or at any time.

'Won't you let me try and see,' pleaded Emily. 'Oh, please let me try.'

'Even if you did change it would be hopeless. No one would think you're me, you are much too small, and besides you have got brown hair.'

'Charlotte, will you really change again? Suppose you couldn't? What will happen while we go to lodgings again and there isn't this bed?

Suppose you got stuck here, and Clare there in your time. Just suppose you did?'

Emily sounded anxious now. Charlotte wanted to reassure her. 'We won't get stuck,' she said. 'Of course we won't get stuck.'

# CHAPTER SIX

I T was Emily who discovered the loose knob on one of the posts at the head of Charlotte's bed. When she unscrewed it she found that the post was hollow.

'Look,' she said, 'Oh, *look*. You could hide things in there. It would make a ripping hiding place.'

But Charlotte, half-asleep, had not been especially interested. 'You had better put the knob back,' she said, 'before Nurse Gregory comes in.'

She awoke two days later to find Emily tugging at her. 'Wake up, wake *up*. Unscrew the knob and look at what's inside the bedpost.'

A sleepy Charlotte was not much inclined to do anything in the chilly room, except huddle on her clothes as fast as she could. In the end Emily unscrewed the bedknob for her. 'Now look,' she said.

For the sake of peace Charlotte clambered on to the bed again, and peered unenthusiastically down into the hollow post. And there was something inside, rolled up and jammed right down, so that she had difficulty in getting hold of it to pull it out; a thin wartime exercise book, Clare's diary.

'You see,' said Emily. 'Now you and Clare can write notes to each other quite safely. She was afraid Nurse Gregory might read them otherwise.'

When Charlotte opened it, careful to avert her eyes from the earlier pages, just as she had promised, she read in Clare's neat writing:

*Dear Charlotte,*

*Did Emily tell you about the bed? I think she might be right, though I did not tell her so. We should be moving to lodgings now quite soon. We must make quite sure I am in 1918, not you, the day we move. Emily would be so worried if you got caught then, and I in your time, and I would be so worried about her.*

*Yours sincerely, Clare.*

This Monday there was no sign of Bunty at breakfast.

'That rotten Miss Wilkin, she told,' Emily said. 'You know, about playing soldiers in the park on Saturday. Poor old Bunty's in fearful trouble now.'

'You were just as bad as Bunty,' Charlotte pointed out.

'I know, wasn't I lucky not to be seen first?' said Emily.

At prayers, Ruth was subdued, rather red-eyed, as if she had been crying. Miss Wilkin looked unhappy too, twisting her engagement ring. Bunty seemed more cheerful than either of them, even though she had to sit on the platform with the staff. She grinned and wriggled on her chair, while Charlotte wondered how she could endure the embarrassment of being there at all, before all those eyes, let alone so cheerfully.

After Miss Bite had read out to the school her usual reports about the war she spoke of Bunty in extremest gravity and sorrow. She was a tall, solemn lady, who made no attempts at jollity like Charlotte's own headmistress, Miss Bowser. She wore a high, old-fashioned collar and steel-rimmed spectacles. The only exception to severity was her hair which she wore piled on her head, but which being very thick and abundant edged its way out of an armoury of pins.

Bunty, she said, had let the school down, let herself down and the girls she had led astray; let her country down in these grave days; disgraced herself, her school, her King, her country.

'The way she spoke, anyone would think Bunty had been rude to God,' said Emily at the mid-morning break.

'Emily,' cried Charlotte, 'you mustn't say things like that.'

But though she was shocked she wondered, disconcertingly, if she would have been quite so shocked if she had not known Clare would be. And Emily said gleefully, 'You rise just like Clare when I say that sort of thing, except that I think she'd have said it was wicked to say that too. I wondered if you'd rise. That's why I said it, as a matter of fact. Anyone would think you were the same person, wouldn't they?'

Even so, when someone handed Charlotte a letter, Emily snatched it away, and ran off by herself to read it, crying over her shoulder. 'It's my letter from my father, and Clare's, but not yours at all. You're not to look at it.'

Charlotte walked on alone along a gravel path. It was dry again this morning yet much less warm, with some scent in the air that made her feel curiously sad. For the first time she was glad of her thick school clothes. She had woken briefly in the night to hear the wind blow, and had not known which time she had heard it in, her own time or the past. But there was certainly a wind today. It had blown the orange leaves from the ends of chestnut branches and yellow ones from the edge of the limes. It blew them along the path towards her with little dry rustling sounds, until she turned into shelter round the corner of the school buildings and met Elsie Brand, crying over a letter.

'Are you all right, Elsie?' she asked anxiously.

'Yes,' said Elsie Brand.

'Are you sure?'

'*Yes*,' said Elsie sniffing. Charlotte walked with her for a while, to keep her company, but need not have bothered for all the notice Elsie took.

Elsie Brand was a very ugly girl. She had big uneven teeth and dust-coloured hair. She had a nose big enough, Bunty said, to hang out a flag on.

Neither Bunty, kind as she usually was, nor anyone else made the slightest effort to be nice to her.

'Her name is Brandt really, not Brand. Her father's German, you see,' Bunty had told Charlotte and Emily conspiratorially. 'My mother says all Germans ought to be interned, they're all spies these days, even the ones who've been here years and years.'

'You must be careful what you say in front of her,' whispered Ruth. 'She might send letters to Germany and tell them things.'

'Whatever sort of things would she have to tell?' asked Emily.

'Well, if you said my father was with the army in France, she might write that.'

'Well, that's silly, they don't need spies to tell them there's an army in France. Anyway, no one can send letters to Germany.'

'And all our letters from here are read too,' added Charlotte.

'She could write them in code though, and her mother could send them on by submarine.'

'I thought you said her father was German not her mother.'

'Her mother must like Germans or she wouldn't have married one.'

'Well, I think it's silly. My Aunt Dolly says all this talk of spies is silly. They'd never have let

Elsie come to school if she was a spy. Besides she's much too ugly,' said Emily.

'She's not really very ugly, Emily,' protested Charlotte.

'My mother says there are spies everywhere and you can't be too careful,' said Bunty.

Despite all the care they took, mistakes were bound to happen now and then in such peculiar circumstances. Teachers had been lenient with their mistakes at first, since Clare and Charlotte were new to school, but they became increasingly less lenient. Once, between the two of them, they forgot a Latin exercise, and another time both Charlotte and Clare drew a map of Africa for Miss Wilkin's geography class, to Miss Wilkin's puzzlement.

Worse of all, perhaps, were the piano lessons. Clare had already been learning the piano for four years, Charlotte barely for a year, and though Clare said she tried to play badly in her lessons she must often have forgotten, judging by the way the teachers reacted to Charlotte's playing.

'You'd almost have thought, Charlotte,' said her own teacher, exasperatedly, 'that you had changed into different people from one lesson to the next.'

Clare's teacher said nothing. She wore ties like a man's and brown suits made of pinstriped cloth. She was white and old and rigid as a bone and she rapped bones, knuckles, hard with a ruler when fingers erred. Charlotte's knuckles she rapped at all the time. Charlotte dreaded her music lessons, although she was learning to play scales faster than it might have been possible otherwise, practising furiously in the narrow draughty cells that were used as practice rooms.

She felt she had to island herself now more and more, to draw in bridges, like a knight barricading himself into his castle. Otherwise she might give herself away, asking a question, for instance, about something she ought to have known if she spent every day in the same place and time, or doing or saying something that would look odd because serious, conscientious Clare would never do or say such things.

This vigilance was tiring. Charlotte began longing to be by herself for a while. It was impossible ever to be alone in Clare's school. But in her own every day, they had more than half an hour to change after games before work started again.

One afternoon she dressed herself as fast as she could.

'Would it matter if I went outside in the garden for a bit?' she asked Elizabeth, who she thought might be less inquisitive than the rest.

'Goodness, whatever do you want to go out for?' asked the sharp-eared Vanessa.

'I'll come with you, if you like,' Susannah offered kindly.

'No, it's all right, thank you, honestly.'

'Of course she wants to go alone,' said Vanessa. 'Charlotte never wants to do anything with anyone else.'

'I want to be alone,' cried Elizabeth, suddenly jumping about the room and chanting it. 'I want to be a-l-o-n-e, want to be a-l-o-n-e,' giggling loudly in between, disconcerting Charlotte, who was not yet used to her sudden turns from silence into buffoonery. But in the disapproving attention this drew from both Janet and Vanessa she was able, quietly, to escape outside.

She did not feel comfortable until a wall of shrubs hid her from the eyes of the school buildings, and then, to her surprise she found herself overcome by a happiness so intense it made her tremble, and at the same time sharpened all her senses.

The September sun was marmalade colour on the brick wall that divided garden from river, reminding her of home, of Aviary Hall. Why, she wondered, should remembering home make you so happy one time, so miserable another. A wren sounded out near by, its sharp song ending in a clock-like buzz. Another one answered it farther off. Charlotte sang too, under her breath, wanting to sing more loudly but not daring to, letting herself out instead in a series of leaps and gallops, more suited, she thought, to someone of Emily's age, but exciting all the same.

The thickening bushes slowed her down at last. She pushed tentatively among them, expecting to find herself in a cave of leaves and twigs, but emerged instead into the strangest kind of garden, very overgrown. All its trees and bushes were curiously shaped and coloured; little flattened trees with twisted branches and red and feathery leaves, the redness too pink to be merely an autumn colour; coppery bushes with long leaves, others with sprays of round leaves, widely spaced, all seeming to absorb the sun's warmth and light and reflect it back again. Set among them was a pond of thick black water half covered in lily leaves, the midges wavering over it in a cloud and dragonflies flicking like little helicopters. There was a bridge very steeply humped, many slats and railings gone, the rest showing faded and blistered remains of dark pink paint. On the far side of it, leaning on one of the only firm-looking pieces of rail, there stood, staring at the water, a tall fair girl.

Charlotte stepped back at once seeing her, reluctant to explain herself, especially to a senior girl as this one seemed. She was uncertain in any case whether she should be here or not, whether it was out of bounds. But the layer of leaves and twigs from the bushes spat beneath her feet, and the tall fair girl turned round.

'Hullo,' she said. 'It's Charlotte, isn't it?' It was Sarah. Her voice sounded much nearer than the bridge looked. Perhaps in the late slanted sunlight the lake gave merely an illusion of size. 'Wait a minute, will you? I'm just coming.' Sarah was with Charlotte quickly, just half a dozen steps, it seemed, from the centre of the bridge, including the leap she had to make over its gaping holes.

'Well, how is it going?' she asked, flicking scraps of paint from her dark-blue skirt, looking at Charlotte in an intent and curious way.

'Very well, thank you,' replied Charlotte uncertainly. Someone whose expression was so hard to interpret was not someone to make you feel at ease, especially when they stared at you as hard, as strangely as Sarah stared. Charlotte's head had begun to prickle, the midges having begun to bite. It was a relief almost when an aeroplane buried them in sound, so making talk impossible.

'It's supposed to be Japanese, this garden,' said Sarah abruptly, when silence fell once more. 'No one has touched it for years, of course.'

She hesitated. 'Come on, we ought to go or you'll be late for prep.'

Again Charlotte had the feeling there was something Sarah wanted to say, other than what she actually said.

Sarah knew the path out of the garden and they went along it, but without hurry. It was almost the first time since she came to school that Charlotte had been alone with someone other than Susannah or Emily, and there came over her a sudden huge longing to tell Sarah about what was happening. She half stopped, opened her mouth, turned towards her, but the sight of that remote pale face checked her. She could have spoken to air, perhaps, but not now to anyone she was looking at.

Sarah, however, stopped suddenly. Gazing straight in front of her, still without turning to Charlotte, she said quickly, determinedly, 'My mother told me to be kind to you, Charlotte, if you came.'

'Your mother,' said Charlotte amazed. 'But I don't know your mother.' In case that sounded rude, as if she meant she would hate to know her, she added less emphatically, 'At least, I don't think I do.'

Sarah turned her head and gazed at Charlotte with unmoving eyes. She smiled a little even. 'I don't think she knows you either. She never said that. She just told me that if a girl called Charlotte Makepeace came to school I was to be kind to her. She's never told me to be kind to anyone else.'

That evening Susannah asked Charlotte to be her best friend. No one had ever asked her this before, and though certain she did not really want to be Susannah's best friend she was touched and pleased by it. Nor did she know how to refuse without being unkind. In the end therefore she answered yes, but she was so busy thinking about what Sarah had said to her in the afternoon that she forgot to mention Susannah when she wrote to Clare in the pink-covered exercise book.

Earlier she had tried, idly, to unscrew the knob at the head of the bed, thinking it might be better to store the pink exercise book inside the post too. It would be safer there she thought. She did not entirely trust Janet or Vanessa not to read it if they ever had the chance.

But as she tugged at it the door opened and Janet came in. So she left it abruptly, and laid the exercise book in its usual place on the chair beside the bed.

# CHAPTER SEVEN

CHARLOTTE had barely fallen asleep when a whistle penetrated her dream, shrilling on and on though she shook her head and groaned to make it stop.

She opened her eyes at last to find everything still dark.

'Wake up, Clare,' someone was saying. 'Wake up at once!'

But the darkness hid all differences. She could not tell at first where or when she was.

'Wake *up*,' insisted the figure beside her bed, shaking her, prodding with her voice. 'Wake up, Clare,' it went on repeating, until gradually Charlotte began to realize that the name called was Clare not Charlotte.

'What's the time?' she asked sleepily. 'What's the matter?'

'Air raid alarm. Hurry up.' Nurse Gregory was brisk. 'Quickly, find your dressing gown.'

Charlotte and Emily were sent into the passages, now only dimly lit, were swept into a tide of girls in dressing gowns, sleepy-looking, their voices hushed, their slippers whispering on linoleum, with none of the daytime clatter and noise. It was hard to tell voices from feet as they slipped downstairs, along more passages, to the gymnasium. They lined up in rows beneath the eyes of Miss Bite their headmistress, who wore a dressing gown and had her hair in a thick plait down her back.

The gym looked bleak, was meanly lit. The clustered ropes made shadows near the ceiling like huge upturned spiders, swaying a little now and then, though there seemed to be no wind below where Charlotte stood. Perhaps so many people breathing made them move, she thought, watching the shadow spiders, watching the two shadow stripes above the parallel bars bend and dart. One wall of the gym was more thickly striped, by the wall bars and their shadows alternately. When the lights moved so did they, and the wooden bars looked no more solid to the eye than the shadows behind them on the wall.

It made an expectancy for her, a fear. The war had never frightened Charlotte much before – to her surprise, for she had thought you always would be frightened in a war – but it frightened her now. Would planes really come? Would bombs really fall on them?

Nothing happened, though. Miss Bite read the registers class by class, the buzz of names and answers not echoing from the roof so much as disappearing slowly, melting, like the sounds in a vaulted church. Charlotte was lulled by it. Dazed and sleepy still she felt she floated high above everyone.

She could not remember whether to listen for Makepeace or Moby so failed to answer any name at all till prodded by Emily when Moby had been called three times.

'Yes . . . yes, Miss Bowser,' she called, confusedly, and could not understand the giggles around.

Would bombs really fall? Would they fall on her she went on wondering less and less urgently. But Miss Bite closed the registers with a snap and announced, a false alarm, a mere practice for the real thing – blowing a whistle for the all-clear to send them shuffling, disconsolately, disappointedly even, back to bed.

They were still forbidden to talk. But when no one was looking, Bunty crept up to Emily and hissed disgustedly what a cheat it was, how in a real raid they would have had cocoa and biscuits and stayed downstairs much longer, listening to stories and singing funny songs.

'I wish it had been real,' Emily said longingly afterwards, as she and Charlotte lay awake. 'It sounds such awful fun. Bunty saw a plane shot down once, she wasn't supposed to look out but she did, it was like a little red flame falling. I wish I could see one too. There weren't any air raids where Aunt Dolly lived.'

'I wouldn't want to,' said Charlotte. For there would have been people inside the little red flame and it might have fallen on the school, on them.

'Oh, you're feeble, just like Clare. I don't suppose I'll see one now anyway. Bunty's father says the war will end quite soon, she says.'

Later, she said sleepily, 'Didn't Miss Bite look funny in a dressing gown and with that silly plait like a little girl. Do you know, her slipper fell off once when she got down off the platform and I saw her bare toes!'

'I don't suppose they were so much different from anyone else's toes,' said Charlotte. But Emily went on giggling till she fell asleep.

In the morning Charlotte still felt confused and her head ached after the interrupted night. She sat for some time in the preparation class, trying to sort out what work she had to do; but even then did not remember she had to learn a poem for Miss Bowser's poetry class on Monday morning. She had two detentions in the afternoon, for an arithmetic question as well as the forgotten Latin exercise, and went to bed that night so tired she could scarcely speak, quite forgetting again to tell Clare about Susannah being her best friend.

When she awoke next day it was raining. The cedar tree gave rain a different, special sound, a kind of hiss and bounce, which mingled with the other sounds, some soft, some clear, of its pouring, dripping, running. The drenched earth outside smelt clean and bold as a knife.

Clare's diary was hidden as usual inside the bedpost. Charlotte read there what she had been expecting to read for days, and did not know what she felt about it, whether she was pleased or sad.

Miss Bite called me in to see her. We're to move on Friday. The people are called Chisel Brown. Friday is my day here in 1918, so that is all right.

Emily was still asleep. Charlotte felt extraordinarily fond of her. If the Mobys moved on Friday and Emily was right about the bed being the reason for their changing about, she would see her for two days more and then never, never again.

A while later it occurred to her that even for Sunday she had been lying awake some considerable time. Surely the bell should be ringing soon? She prodded at Emily, who was beginning to wake of her own accord, grunting, sighing, humping up the bed clothes.

'Emily. *Emily.* Isn't it very late? Isn't it time for the bell?'

'No, it isn't. Don't you remember we've an extra hour?' Emily sounded extremely cross, not living up to the softness Charlotte had been feeling towards her.

'How do you mean, an extra hour?'

'Oh, it's you. I thought it was Clare. Don't they do that with you any more, put the clocks on for summertime, and then back in the autumn?'

'Oh yes, but not yet.'

'Well, they've done it here, and you've woken me up for nothing, bother you.'

'You were beginning to wake up already.'

'No, I *wasn't*. I was fast asleep.'

Charlotte let it go. She did not feel like an argument.

Next morning Vanessa had to shake her awake. For she had one hour's less sleep than usual, two hours less than the night before. All the rest of that week there continued this curious affair of nights longer and shorter than usual, alternately – the effect quite as disconcerting as it would be suddenly to find yourself walking on legs of different lengths, or seeing with different sighted eyes.

Charlotte always seemed to be sleepy. She wished she could make up for the shorter nights by extra sleep on the longer nights, but never succeeded, lying awake instead each early morning for what seemed hours, listening to Emily's even breathing and thinking thoughts about what might happen which she would have preferred not to have time to think. After each shorter night on the other hand Vanessa and company continued having to shake her out of sleep.

Probably her sleepiness and consequent confusion were part of the reason why everything began to seem impossibly wrong. As early as Monday she was overwhelmed. It was the morning of Miss Bowser's poetry class and only five minutes before it was due to begin Charlotte realized that she had forgotten to learn a poem for it. There was no time now. She could only hope she would not be asked to recite.

Unfortunately, Miss Bowser chose this day to test her new girls – just Charlotte and Susannah in their class. Susannah had her name called first and stood giggling to recite Tennyson's *Brook*, each word in it given the same weight as the one before and the one after, each line plodded out in procession, sounding more like a wheel than water.

'That's enough, Sue. Well done,' said Miss Bowser. 'Sit down now.' She was quite different from solemn, old-fashioned, remote Miss Bite. She was tall, smart and stoutish, and wore pink-rimmed spectacles and pink lipstick and usually suits of tweed. She had a jolly smile, inviting confidence. 'Just because I'm headmistress don't be afraid of me,' it seemed to say. But because she was the headmistress most people were afraid.

Neither Janet nor Vanessa spoke in her classes unless invited to, though they shouted all the time in most other ones.

'Well now, Charlotte,' she asked encouragingly. 'What have you got for us? Eh?'

Charlotte climbed reluctantly to her feet. During Susannah's poem she had remembered with relief *How Horatius Kept the Bridge*, and repeated the verses over in her head. She began in a rush.

'*Lars Porsena of Clusium* . . .'

'Give us the title first please, dear,' said Miss Bowser. 'We all like to hear the title first, you know.'

'*How Horatius Kept the Bridge*,' began Charlotte again, less fast but very loud, louder indeed than she had meant, so she lowered her voice almost to a whisper for the first line of the poem.

'*Lars Porsena of Clusium,*
   *By the nine gods he swore* . . .'

Miss Bowser was looking at her, still smiling. Charlotte gazed past at the blackboard, which had the date written on it beautifully, in two colours.

*'That the Proud House of Tarquin . . .'*

Miss Bowser broke in. 'Do you have your book, Charlotte, the one I asked you to choose a poem from?'

Charlotte nodded. It lay on her desk – *A New Anthology for the Middle School.*

'Do you mind showing me your poem there?'

Charlotte felt suddenly afraid; though taking the book she searched with some hopelessness still through the index of first lines. But there was no sign of *Lars Porsena of Clusium.* Hurriedly she turned to the index of titles, leafing the pages over to find *How Horatius Kept the Bridge.* There was no sign of that either. Miss Bowser watched her, smiling all the time, the smile trapped on her face now, not jolly any more. She was touching her pink smile with pink-painted fingernails. Charlotte had begun to leaf through the book itself, hoping, still hoping, but more and more hopelessly.

'Have you found it yet, Charlotte?' Miss Bowser enquired.

'No . . . no, I haven't,' replied Charlotte, blushing and trembling.

'That doesn't surprise me, dear,' said Miss Bowser, 'since it is not in the book.' She paused impressively. She put both hands down on the teaching desk and leaned forward over them, angled like a figurehead of a ship, as hefty, as stern. She was not smiling now.

'I suppose, Charlotte, that was a poem you learnt at your last school and were hoping to palm off on stupid Miss Bowser as this week's work?' This was so nearly true – if also miles off in a way Miss Bowser could never have guessed – that Charlotte had no defence. She stood miserably, almost in tears, lifting one hand to push back her hair and feeling her face grow hotter and hotter.

'I'm nothing like as stupid as that, you know, Charlotte. Am I, girls?'

'No, Miss Bowser,' they chorused, all eyes on her, but creeping now and then slyly to Charlotte, with sympathy or enjoyment or disapproval.

Miss Bowser took fire. She could take it, evangelistically, on almost anything from moral standards to lost property or untidy cloakrooms, steering her voice as skilfully as at other times she steered her car.

'You have been very lazy, Charlotte, very deceitful, very stupid. I don't like any of these things. I don't like the laziness of work not done. I don't like the deceit that tries to disguise such laziness. I don't like the stupidity you have shown, Charlotte, in trying to disguise both laziness and deceit.

'You are one of the oldest in this class, you know, and you came to us with good reports. But now I hear only bad reports of you; work forgotten, work slackly done. I hear you had no less than two detentions on Saturday, which for a new girl is a disgrace. What is more, I hear you are unfriendly, do not join in and take part with the other girls, and that is something we do not like in this school. You let yourself down by this behaviour, you know, Charlotte. You let your class down, you let me down, you let the school down. I think you'd better learn the poem on page seventy-nine which begins, *When the British Warrior Queen, Bleeding from the Roman Rods*, since you seem to like the Romans. I'll hear you recite it tomorrow afternoon after lunch.'

Then Miss Bowser took her hands off the table, let her smile break out again.

'Well, Charlotte, I think that's quite enough lecturing for now. Let's have no more trouble, eh?

I like these classes to be a pleasant time for everyone. I don't like trouble any more than you, you know. Eh, Charlotte?'

'Yes, Miss Bite,' observed Charlotte, head bowed over *A New Anthology for the Middle School.*

'I think for a start you might get my name right, Charlotte,' cried Miss Bowser, forgiving her with a jolly laugh.

Everyone was subdued for the rest of the session, not only Charlotte. Afterwards people crowded round. But though they were all sympathetic then, later, upstairs, Charlotte heard Vanessa whispering to Janet how it wouldn't hurt goody Charlotte to be given a proper ticking-off like that, she was so snooty and standoffish usually.

That evening, Charlotte was lying on her bed reading, and trying not to think about what had happened in the morning, when all three of them came to her, Janet, Vanessa and Elizabeth. They stood accusingly round the bed.

'It's not kind,' said Janet.

'It's beastly,' added Vanessa.

'Look, you know, you can't say you'll be someone's best friend and then just not speak to them,' put in Elizabeth indignantly.

'Poor Susie's terribly upset,' explained Janet.

'I mean, if you don't want to be friends with her you must tell her,' cried Elizabeth.

'We don't mind if you don't speak to us,' said Vanessa, 'but you must talk to Susannah, you really must.'

'It isn't fair not to talk to her,' said Janet, 'if she's your best friend.'

Charlotte had been too preoccupied lately to think much about Susannah. But she was overcome now with guilt, remembering that Susannah had looked unhappy and knowing that she had kept on forgetting to tell Clare they were supposed to be such friends.

'I'm sorry. I didn't mean it. I'm sorry,' she said. But before she or the others could say any more, Susannah herself appeared, rather red about the eyes, making Charlotte feel guiltier than ever and setting the rest to give her meaning glances in place of words.

When the lights went out Charlotte lay in bed trying not to cry because everything, everyone, even Elizabeth whom she liked so much, seemed to be against her now. Poor Clare, she thought, must be as confused and miserable, for it followed that they were all against Clare as well.

She was certain what she wanted now. This confusion came from the double life they led, so she longed quite certainly for it to end. She longed for Friday and normality, and though she was sad when Thursday came because she would never see Emily again, it was a kind of numb, remote sadness that stayed outside, unsinking in her mind.

Before they went to sleep that night she asked Emily the question she would never have another chance to ask.

'Emily – are Clare and I – are we so very alike?'

Emily did not answer at once.

'If we're not,' Charlotte said, 'I can't understand why no one noticed that I'm not her and she's not me.'

'It's funny,' Emily said. 'I don't think you are so alike. At least, not in some ways. It was just that . . . Well, you see, I just expected to see Clare and so I thought it was. And of course you pretended you were Clare.'

'I didn't pretend exactly. You kept on calling me Clare and I didn't see how I could explain I wasn't.'

'Then you *did* pretend,' said Emily provokingly.

'You wouldn't have believed me if I had told you.' Charlotte grew annoyed, to her own surprise, because she did not mean to feel annoyance. 'You didn't believe it for ages, even when you knew something funny was happening. Oh, I'm sorry, Emily, I didn't mean to quarrel, not tonight.'

'I wasn't quarrelling,' said Emily. '*I* didn't say *anything.*'

'I know, it was just me, really, getting cross,' said Charlotte apologetically.

Emily said, 'I don't suppose I ever looked at you properly – or Clare. I mean, I knew you – her – too well, at least I thought I did, perhaps that's why I never noticed you were different.'

Perhaps we never look at people properly, Charlotte thought. She remembered looking in a mirror once and trying to draw herself, how after she had been staring at them for a little while her features seemed no longer to make her face or any face. They were just a collection of eyes and nose and mouth. Perhaps if you stared at anyone like that their faces would disintegrate in the same way, till you could not tell whether you knew them or not, especially, of course, if there was no reason for them not to be who they said they were.

And, she thought uncomfortably, what would happen if people did not recognize you? Would you know who you were yourself? If tomorrow they started to call her Vanessa or Janet or

Elizabeth, would she know how to be, how to feel like, Charlotte? Were you some particular person only because people recognized you as that?

Next day felt strange, an unwinding and relief. But though Charlotte was certain she would not go back in time again, she felt flat as well as relieved, anxious to grab at anything to remind herself of Emily and Clare. She was delighted when the school walk that afternoon set off in the direction of the church by the river, to which she had never been in her own time, for the school had had a chapel built since 1918 and all the Sunday services were now held there. She had liked the church with its plain round-topped windows and blue starred ceiling and found the thought of its continuity comforting today.

Vanessa and Janet and Susannah were playing games that afternoon, and so Charlotte walked with Elizabeth, of whom she still felt shy, especially after Monday's lecturing. Elizabeth had holes in both her stockings and white marks on her skirt.

When they came to the river the island looked like a ship moored upon it with golden trees growing round its decks. There was the little dock too, just as Charlotte remembered it with its barges and small squat crane. There was the church . . . She looked for it eagerly and found the shape ahead of them, but drawing nearer saw to her horror that it was no longer the whole, roofed-in solid church, just walls and a few distorted beams. The doors had been boarded up and willow-herb and thistles grew around. She stopped abruptly to stare at it. Elizabeth stopped too and so did the couple behind them.

Charlotte said, almost in tears, 'But I thought . . . I didn't know it was like this. I thought . . .'

'What did you think?' asked Elizabeth. They had begun to walk again, slowly, lagging behind the rest.

'It had a roof – I mean it was a proper church. Not like this.'

The bricks were blackened where the roof had been. There was jagged blackened glass round the edges of the windows. On some the frames were still more or less complete.

'But it's been burnt down for years,' Elizabeth said. 'Oh, for ages, I think.'

'But I *saw* a roof,' cried Charlotte, 'and it was all blue with little gold stars on it.' She did not think about betraying herself, and briefly she did not care. After all it did not much matter now.

'But, look, you couldn't have seen a roof,' Elizabeth was saying, hotly. 'It must have been burnt long before you were born, so you couldn't have seen it, could you, not possibly, not unless you'd been been alive before . . .'

Elizabeth was joking, Charlotte thought. She could not have meant that seriously. Yet it gave her another chance to tell, and suddenly she wanted to; but she could not, could not frame the words. Supposing Elizabeth did not believe her? She only said, lamely, 'Someone must have told me – about the gold stars I mean. Or . . . or perhaps I dreamed it. I don't know.'

Elizabeth said, 'Hm. Hmmm.' She stared at Charlotte intently, while Charlotte went on pretending not to know she stared, looking straight ahead of her, though she was beyond thinking of something nonchalant to say.

'I can't make you out. Look, why are you so strange? Why do you say such odd, such peculiar things? As if you never listened, never noticed anything that went on. Honestly, I wonder about you sometimes.'

She stopped staring at Charlotte, fiddled about with her untidy hair, making it untidier, pulled her skirt round and tried to rub the white marks off it with a wetted finger.

'There is something, isn't there – something odd? Look, look, why don't you tell? I wouldn't tell anyone else, I promise, if you told. Honestly I wouldn't. *Honestly.*'

Charlotte, stunned by now, shook her head, still not looking at Elizabeth who would have argued more. But to Charlotte's great relief the prefect in charge called out and walking back to hurry them, became involved in some other argument with Elizabeth which they carried on all the way home. Between Charlotte and Elizabeth nothing more was said, though Charlotte thought a great deal. The church still upset her considerably. She found she did not want to talk about it to Elizabeth or anyone.

That evening in their room they had a pillow fight, started by Elizabeth. All of them joined in, even Charlotte, free of Clare as she thought, of solemn Clare, but still tentative, being out of practice at fooling about. Susannah was excited, jumping up and down, yelling for the pillow to be thrown at her, missing it usually if it was thrown and giggling almost too much to throw it back. Elizabeth swung alive in her sudden astonishing way, pretended to dance with pillows or box with them, throwing wildly, knocking ornaments and photographs off the chests-of-drawers. Janet and Vanessa, on the other hand, threw with a careful, deadly accuracy as if they were playing school games.

In the middle of the fight the door opened and Sarah walked in to lecture them coldly, Charlotte as the rest, without a sign of friendliness, which hurt Charlotte a little. But as Sarah went out of the room again, she had a sudden, wild, extraordinary idea about her. Why had she never thought of such a thing before?

'Elizabeth,' she asked, 'Elizabeth, what's her name?'

'Sarah, of course, idiot.'

'No, silly, her surname, I mean.'

Elizabeth was reading again and did not answer at once. Charlotte almost brought an answer out herself, had the name ready on her lips; *Moby* it was, for that name would explain everything.

'Reynolds,' said Elizabeth. 'Her name's Reynolds, didn't you know?'

Charlotte had known, of course, had just lost the name temporarily. Had it been Moby she would have noticed at once on school lists, she realized, as she had noticed Reynolds, although the name Reynolds meant nothing to her. Five minutes before she had not been excited or expectant at all, but now she felt as hugely disappointed as if she had waited a week for Elizabeth's answer, expecting to find out from it why Sarah's mother knew her name, and even a little about Emily or Clare grown up.

When she thought about it, Charlotte half dreaded the ordinariness of waking next to Susannah for the second morning running. She found herself still dreading it next morning as she swam up out of sleep, so lay for a moment with closed eyes, the sunshine rosy on her lids, until suddenly she realized there should be no sun and felt after all a surge of hope. Perhaps she and Clare would continue to change after all on alternate days, lodgings or no lodgings. But when she opened her eyes she saw the cedar tree as before, and the 1918 school bedroom. She started up abruptly.

Emily lay beside her, but at Charlotte's movement she too, awoke and sat up blinking, gazing at Charlotte first with bewilderment and then, increasingly, with horror.

'But I thought . . .' Charlotte said. 'I thought . . .'

Emily spoke in a small flat voice. 'We didn't go into lodgings yesterday after all. We're going today.'

# PART TWO

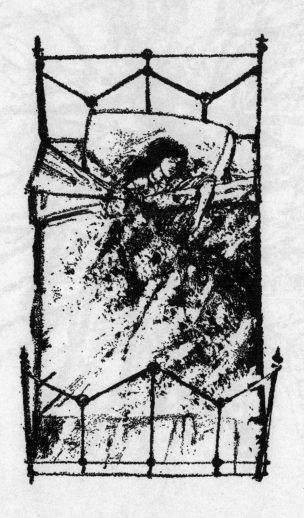

# CHAPTER ONE

AFTER a long pause Charlotte said, 'Why, Emily?'

'They didn't say why. They just said we were going on Saturday after all, not Friday. They just said it.'

'Did Clare . . . ?'

'Clare tried to sleep in another bed, to stop her changing with you. But Nurse Gregory caught her. Clare had a fearful wigging. She hates rows and she said she'd better wait a bit before trying again. I suppose she must have just gone to sleep. You and she have been very sleepy haven't you, all this week?'

'Perhaps we'll go on changing, lodgings or no lodgings . . . ?'

'I don't believe that. I don't. It's silly.'

'I should have slept on the floor or something, just to make sure,' said Charlotte desperately.

'Oh, don't be silly.'

'Perhaps they'll hold us up again – and we'll – you'll stay here till tomorrow.'

'Of course we'll go today. They said we would.'

'Oh, Emily, please don't cry.'

'Leave me alone, oh leave me alone. I don't want you to talk to me.'

After breakfast the trunks were brought out. Clare's was an old black tin one with brass studs round the edge, its paint chipped, its tin dented. Emily's was brown with a wooden frame, and looked as if dust had settled on it years ago and stuck. Nurse Gregory stood over them while they packed, her arms folded in like steel rods, not seeming pleased to have her sickroom empty after all, for almost the only thing she said, apart from telling them how badly they packed, was what a pity it was they were going because they badly needed the discipline only she could give.

The school pony trap came for them sharp at eleven o'clock. Nurse Gregory stood on the portico to see Charlotte and Emily go, granting each a ration of her steely smile. It was only then, too late, Charlotte remembered she had not rescued Clare's diary from its hiding place.

In almost any other circumstances Charlotte would have enjoyed the drive to Flintlock Lodge, watching the swaying shiny quarters of the pony, catching the wind's small bite upon her face while the trap creaked and jiggled under her. But she was much too worried to enjoy anything. She was worried about Emily, who sat white and fixed-looking, staring ahead of them, and who since they first awoke had scarcely said a word. It seemed wrong that a girl of ten should be so coldly and silently controlled. But she was worried too about her own predicament, increasingly desolate, wondering if she would ever see her sister Emma again, or her grandfather, Elijah, or her home, Aviary Hall. If she stayed in this time as Clare and grew up as her, she would be a woman of nearly sixty when Emma was still only twelve. Emma would never recognize her grown so old; might not want to recognize her, thought Charlotte miserably.

Somehow they would have to change places again, she and Clare. She would have to sleep at school in the bed with the little wheels. But how?

But how? She looked at Emily still gazing rigidly and tried to will the idea into her that all would be well eventually, that Clare would return to her. But Emily's face never stirred. Charlotte did not at this moment feel much hope herself. And Clare, she wondered, what about Clare, whatever was she feeling now?

Flintlock Lodge was not a house to make anyone feel more cheerful. Tall and thin and grey, it had a pointed gable to one side of it, a big bay window jutting out below. It needed paint like all the other houses around, and its garden needed pruning like the other gardens, and like the trees that stood along the road. At the back stood a monkey-puzzle tree, taller even than the house.

Inside, the house was less shabby than outside, but very dark, because of the trees and creepers crowded outside, and because the furniture was all so dark, blackish even, but with a dim shine on it like treacle. It was huge too, chests and cupboards and cabinets for giants, a clock like a church tower, ticking like a drum. In the dining room the chairs were so huge and cold and slippery, that Charlotte felt like Goldilocks on Father Bear's outsize chair. She needed to wriggle to make herself comfortable but did not dare. A great black dresser stood opposite her place, angled and bracketed all over, more black objects standing on its brackets and some green and pink and turquoise vases of glass with fluted edges. Between two of these she saw a photograph of a boy, slightly tinted and in an ebony frame.

She wondered who the boy was. She stared at him during most of the meal, for there was nowhere else for her to look. Emily just turned her face away from eyes, the shiny cat and little hairy dog lay hidden beneath the table, breathing wheezily, and it seemed rude to stare at Mr and Mrs Chisel Brown or their daughter Miss Agnes Chisel Brown.

Mrs Chisel Brown, however, stared at Charlotte and Emily. She stared without saying a word until the food came in, when she stared at that instead, craning round to see Miss Agnes dish it out, and then pursuing the plate with her eyes from the sideboard to her place. She ate so quickly that Charlotte had barely touched her plate before Mrs Chisel Brown's was empty, showing a crack across it, glued, also clamped with little metal claws.

'Too much salt, Aggie,' she said in a fat voice, wiping a napkin across her mouth. She wore a black dress with a shine on it almost like the furniture's. 'Poor mutton too.'

'It's the war, you see, Mother. Meat is very scarce, you know, and the butcher did save this particularly.'

'The war, the war. What will they do afterwards to excuse poor mutton?'

'Up at the hospital yesterday,' ventured Miss Agnes, 'they were saying, I told you, the news is quite hopeful now of peace.'

'Damned peace talk, damned conchies, hun-lovers. Should all be hanged, I say,' said Mr Chisel Brown. He had white hair, white brows and a white moustache struck across his bright-red face, like a Christmas parcel with white ribbon round it. He looked and sounded a military man, more Colonel or Major than plain Mr Chisel Brown. He did not speak to Charlotte and Emily at all, conveyed messages merely through his daughter, Miss Agnes.

'Hope Misses Moby know there's a war on, use gas, water, patriotically.'

'You will remember not to use too much hot water, to light the gas in your room only when necessary, won't you, dear,' explained Miss Agnes anxiously.

'Yes,' said Charlotte; and, 'Yes,' muttered Emily.

'Mean, yes, Miss Agnes Chisel Brown,' boomed Mr Chisel Brown.

'Yes, Miss Agnes Chisel Brown, you ought to say,' Miss Agnes whispered across to them.

'Yes, Miss Agnes Chisel Brown,' whispered Charlotte back, but Emily said no more.

'Young ladies these days, Hunnish manners, seemingly,' observed Mr Chisel Brown wiping his moustache. 'Arthur, a lad, behaved quite differently.'

In Charlotte and Emily's bedroom hung a picture called 'Mark of the German Beast', which showed a huge, glowering face drawn in brown pencil. But the eyes were gun holes for shooting at unarmed men; the ears crouched women with murdered babies in their arms; the nose, the mouth, the chin all represented horrors. They were what Charlotte saw first when she opened her eyes next day. Therefore she was not surprised to see next the perverse, irritating shapes of the monkey-puzzle tree outside the window and not as she had hoped the glaring brick of the new school annexe, which she would have found beautiful today.

'Oh, you're still here, are you?' said Emily casually, leaning over her. 'I told you you would be, didn't I? I said it was that bed that made you change with Clare, I told you so.'

She leapt back on to her bed, which was very high but deep, like a sofa, with no room for even a child to crawl between it and the floor beneath.

'It's much comfier than school beds,' she cried, bouncing vigorously. She might not have been gloomy yesterday at all, to Charlotte's surprise and also her relief.

'Mind out, Emily. Don't bust the springs,' she said.

It was raining today. But the rain had stopped by lunchtime and after lunch Charlotte and Emily were ordered by Mr Chisel Brown, through Miss Agnes, to take the dog out into the garden where dead brown flowers still stood on rhododendron bushes, which must have first flowered in June, and where they could scarcely move without banging into some dripping shrub, so showering themselves uncomfortably. The dog seemed to dislike it quite as much as Charlotte and Emily, lifting his feet disconsolately from the muddy paths. He looked like a millipede, Emily said. The matt of hair hanging down on either side of him was like little, myriad legs.

Before them the monkey-puzzle tree sprang up and out.

'I bet I could climb it,' said Emily.

Charlotte surveyed it doubtfully. 'Well, if you could get up the first part where there aren't any branches.'

'Oh, you'd need a ladder, of course. After that it's like stairs. I bet it's awfully easy if you're good at climbing trees.'

'If the leaves, or whatever you call those spiky green things, are as prickly as they look they'd hurt your hands like anything.'

'Yes, but some of the branches haven't any at all, they're bare, you see. You could miss out the prickly ones, couldn't you?'

It was odd, the way the dark-green spikes seemed to spring straight out from the wood. The trunk too, had its own curious construction, small horizontal ridges at uneven intervals, that would be rough, Charlotte thought, on knees and shins.

'I will climb it one day. I will anyway, you'll see,' said Emily. She was bored now. She kicked the path or threw a stick for the dog to chase, but he continued as droopy at their heels.

'He's such a boring dog. It's all boring. I think it's the most boring place I've ever known. The Chisel Browns are the most boring people.'

'They're just old. That's all, I think,' said Charlotte.

'Aunt Dolly says it isn't polite to talk about the food and stare at it like Mrs Chisel Brown does all the time,' said Emily righteously. 'She calls it pig talk, pig behaviour.'

'You and Bunty talk about the food all the time at school.'

'That's different, we're children. Mrs Chisel Brown's a grown-up lady.'

'It's no different. If you know better, you shouldn't do it.'

'Well, Mrs Chisel Brown must know better and she still does it. That silly Miss Agnes should tell her not to. Don't you think Miss Agnes is silly?'

'Not especially,' said Charlotte primly.

'Well, I do. I think she's one of the silliest people I've ever met. And she's ugly too, uglier even than Elsie Brand.'

'I think you're being horried, Emily,' said Charlotte.

'I think I shall call her Ugly Aggie. Yes, Ugly Aggie, that's a good name.'

Emily laughed loudly and for a long time. Afterwards, though, came an even longer silence. She was looking at Charlotte, who could not make out her face at all. Eventually she said, 'Clare would say it wasn't good or Christian to talk like that. She'd say I ought to say sorry in my prayers.'

'I said you were horrid, didn't I? Anyway I'm not Clare. You know I'm not.' Charlotte picked up a dried rhododendron leaf, brown and tough-looking and curled at the edges, like a boat, she thought, balancing it across her hand.

'I know you're not Clare too,' said Emily loudly. 'But you've got to be her anyway, haven't you? You should just try harder, that's all.'

'Emily, you're being horrid.'

'I feel horrid. I feel horrid. I wish . . . I wish . . .' Emily stopped, scowled, as suddenly laughed and ran away across the lawn and back again.

'We were just talking about your monkey-puzzle tree,' Charlotte said, for Miss Agnes came just then to call them in.

'Isn't it funny, dear? You can see it would puzzle monkeys,' cried Miss Agnes with a bright giggle. She had large teeth and giggling showed them all. Charlotte did not dare look at Emily, saying rather hurriedly, 'Emily thought you could climb it if you had a ladder first.'

'My brother climbed it once as a lad. He borrowed a ladder from the gardener.'

'Didn't you climb it too?' asked Emily.

'Oh no, dear, that would have been most unladylike.'

'I don't care about being ladylike. Is that your brother in the photograph in the dining room?'

'Yes, that is Arthur,' replied Miss Agnes.

'Is he younger than you?'

'Oh yes, by several years. Was younger, I should say.'

'Why, is he dead then?' asked Emily, ignoring the little kick Charlotte gave her as a hint to ask no more questions: it was rude.

'He was killed, dear, in this terrible war. In France.'

'My father's in France too,' said Emily subdued again.

The dog shook itself and sniffed. The trees and bushes dripped noisily. Charlotte was looking at the ground, at the wet scattered leaves, but after a moment she felt Miss Agnes seem to shake herself, saw her unwind her knitted fingers. She heard her say quickly, almost defiantly, as she turned to lead them indoors again, 'We had such a nice letter from the Colonel to say how bravely dear Arthur had died. Of course we knew he had been brave, we'd never doubted it, but it was very kind of him to write and tell us so.'

They went to the dining room, where Charlotte and Emily had been told they might sit each day. Rather awkward-seeming and embarrassed still, Miss Agnes knelt on the floor beside its big black cupboard and opened the lower doors. Out fell, tumbling, some books and boxes, some packages wrapped in tissue paper, out on to the shadowy floor.

'These were ours,' she said. 'Mine and Arthur's. You may play with them, if you like. There's no one else to play with them now.' Then she went away rather hurriedly.

# CHAPTER TWO

HOW strange it was to crouch in the half-dark between heavy table and heavy cupboard, exploring the toys of a generation back, by feel and smell as much as sight. It was absorbing and exciting, also sad, because of the faded worn look they had, but perhaps even more because of their smell, dour and musty, the smell of things left long unused.

Charlotte examined a package first, one wrapped in tissue paper, which had none of the crispness and whiteness of new paper. It was yellowed, soft as muslin, barely hissing as Charlotte unfolded it carefully, layer on layer, both she and Emily growing more curious towards the parcel's core, in which, at last, they found a doll. It had a china face rather chilly to touch, with fat white cheeks and huge, fringed eyes. It had arms and legs of china, but the body was soft, covered in thin leather, colder than cloth yet less cold than china for fingers to explore. It wore a blue silk dress short to the knee and humped a little behind, tied by a pink silk sash, also a hat with a feather in it. It had laced high-heeled boots painted on its legs, and impossibly tiny feet.

'Only a doll, a silly doll. She would have played with dolls, of course, Miss Agnes would, I mean,' said Emily in a disappointed voice.

'Well, what's wrong with that then? I used to play with dolls too. And this is such a lovely one.' Charlotte was examining it delightedly, peering to see each tiny perfect detail of stitching and ornament. 'We never had any as beautiful as this.'

'Clare did,' said Emily unexpectedly. 'She had a doll just like this, only nicer, that belonged to our mother when she was a little girl. It was the only thing we had of hers. She died when I was three, you know, and our father was so sad he sold everything else, all the furniture and all her old toys and books and things. But he let Clare keep the doll.'

'Didn't you have anything yourself?' said Charlotte, looking at her, horrified. She could think of nothing more sad than to have nothing at all to remind you of your mother.

'I had my father's soldiers. He gave them to me specially, he wanted me to play with them. He'd really wanted me to be a boy, you see.'

In spite of all this, after a moment Emily held out her hand for the doll, examining it as carefully as Charlotte had done. She began to undress it; and when Charlotte opening another box found an array of soldiers, once bright blue and red but now rubbed and dented-looking, she gave them at first only a casual glance and continued to fiddle with the tiny hooks and buttons on the doll.

Charlotte explored the other boxes, finding many different games; elaborate jigsaw puzzles, a halma set, draughts in a box made to look like a leather-covered book. Best of all – or so Charlotte thought – in a plain wooden box with a lid that slid in and out, she found a pile of small white sticks, very delicately carved.

Emily by now had left the doll and was arranging and then rearranging the ranks of scarred tin soldiers on the table beneath the light. She jumped as Miss Agnes's hands fell, tentatively, on her shoulders.

'These were dear Arthur's soldiers of course,' she said, making Charlotte jump in her turn. She had not heard Miss Agnes entering either, because engrossed by the small white sticks.

'I didn't think they were *your* soldiers,' said Emily cheekily.

'Emily!' Charlotte nudged her, uncomfortably.

'I wasn't allowed to touch them of course. Arthur said girls should play with dolls instead. But he played with them all the time, you know. They were his favourite toys.'

'I don't like dolls, though I'm a girl. I like playing with soldiers best too, like him.' Emily wriggled a little for Miss Agnes's hands still rested on her back.

'Whatever are those sticks?' she asked Charlotte. 'They look like little baby bones.'

'They're spillikins. It's a sort of game, you see.'

'The spillikins! Why, fancy, the spillikins.' Miss Agnes bent forward excitedly. 'They're made of ivory, of course, and that is bone, Emily.'

Charlotte lifted the box of spillikins and poured them out on to the table. They looked less fragile when defined against the dark wood, but just as delicate, barely thicker than little strips of paper. She arranged them as if she was laying a fire, crisscrossing them, save only for one with a shallow hook on it, that she kept out separately.

'You get the spillikins out with this,' she told Emily. 'If you move two by mistake, then someone else has a turn.'

She was pleased, warm, off her guard, for they had played spillikins at Aviary Hall, she and Emma and sometimes even their grandfather, Elijah. She was still more pleased when Miss Agnes insisted that they all play spillikins now.

To Emily's surprise and indignation Miss Agnes won almost every time. She grew quite pleased and fluttery. Pink spots planted themselves in the centre of each cheek.

'Of course, dears, I always was good at this,' she said. 'I used to beat Arthur every time and he got so cross sometimes, he'd throw them all on the ground, the naughty boy.'

'Well, I'm good at draughts. I can always beat Clare.'

Emily looked at Charlotte pointedly and giggled. But she was much too impatient to be good at spillikins, moving them too fast, not wheedling them out by delicate degrees. Charlotte on the other hand became absorbed, concentrating wholly on her fingers' easing, on the slow light levering of the little strips of bone. There was the moment of suspense when success was near, the relief as she safely flicked a spillikin away, the frustration, contrariwise, when at the last minute fingers lost their control or when one that had seemed an easy win proved so delicately balanced that it set the whole heap twitching at a single touch. The game contracted, expanded seconds, contracted, expanded minutes, made an illusion of no time that lulled Charlotte and comforted her. They might, she thought, have been playing at any time, their minds moving easily from one present to another, from 1918, here, now, to Arthur in the past, to Emma in the future, and also to Clare. This room, she thought, must have looked much the same when Miss Agnes and her brother Arthur were children – the same toys and games were spread about. It might equally have been Aviary Hall as Charlotte knew it, for that had just such dark wood surfaces, just such dowdy light and dim reflections, and saw just such games of spillikins.

She watched Miss Agnes play, her worn fingers moving patiently, her thick brows contracted to a still thicker, blacker line. She felt as if she was suspended between these times, the past, this present, that future of her own, belonging to all and none of them. She looked up half-expecting to see Emma there, besides Miss Agnes, or Arthur, the boy in the tinted photograph. It surprised her to find only Emily.

That night Miss Agnes said they were to go to the drawing room, where Mr and Mrs Chisel Brown stayed all the day as far as Charlotte and Emily could see, though Miss Agnes worked continually, cooking and organizing the house. On one side of its empty fireplace sat Mr Chisel Brown behind his newspaper; on the other, like a fat white Buddha, sat Mrs Chisel Brown behind nothing but her face, which glimmered a little, palely, in the surrounding gloom. The fat hairy dog lay on her lap, the fat black cat was curled up at her feet. On a table beside her stood a forest of photographs. All were of Arthur, Charlotte thought. At least all seemed to be of a boy or man, though she could not see very well and it would have been rude to peer.

'Goodnight,' Charlotte whispered tentatively, for that was what they had come to say.

'Goodnight,' growled Emily.

'My young day,' observed Mr Chisel Brown to his newspaper, 'my young day, young people bade good night each company in turn. Of course, have Hunnish manners now.'

'That's right, dear Emily,' Miss Agnes hinted at their backs. 'Say goodnight, Mr Chisel Brown, Mrs Chisel Brown. Goodnight,' (and here she giggled a little), 'Goodnight, Miss Agnes.'

'Miss Agnes Chisel Brown,' observed her father fiercely.

'Goodnight,' said Charlotte, obedient, confused, and suddenly very, very tired. 'Goodnight, Mr Chisel Brown. Goodnight, Mrs Chisel Brown. Goodnight, Miss Agnes Chisel Brown.'

Emily said nothing, but looked defiantly at Mr Chisel Brown, who rose to his feet and took a soldierly stance, fiddling with his moustache.

'Say goodnight, Emily dear,' Miss Agnes was hinting still.

'Oh please, Emily,' said Charlotte. 'Say goodnight.' Oh please, Emily, she was thinking, please say it, it's so much easier and I'm so tired.

Mr Chisel Brown stared at them, puffing himself out like a balloon, swaying a little on his feet, as if to let the wind carry him away.

Emily gave a little smile. 'Good*night*, Mr Chisel Brown,' she said with almost a curtsey. 'Good*night*, Mrs Chisel Brown. Good*night*, Miss Agnes Chisel Brown. Goodnight, *cat*. Goodnight, *dog*,' she said, and then at once, giggling, fled, out of the drawing room and up the stairs.

Charlotte waited, terrified, her eyes fast to the floor. But nothing happened. Mr Chisel Brown deflated himself and returned to his newspaper. Mrs Chisel Brown continued to sit as she had sat before. Charlotte, beckoned by Miss Agnes, departed at last to her bed. And when she went to breakfast next morning, dreading repercussions, Mr Chisel Brown just glanced over his newspaper with a kind of growl, and nothing more was said that morning or any morning.

'Anyone would think,' said Emily triumphantly, 'anyone would think he was *frightened* to tell me off.'

## CHAPTER THREE

THE following Saturday Emily climbed the monkey-puzzle tree. It had been an odd sort of week for them before Saturday, as day-girls going back and forth to school each day. Things even smelt different, Charlotte thought, from earlier weeks. There was the rather medicinal, disinfectant smell of the day-girls' cloakroom, where they spent quite a lot of their day, changing and gossiping, whereas the boarders' cloakroom, more rarely visited, had smelt of grease and dust and rubber and wet wool. There was also the sad, musty smell of the cupboard in the Chisel Brown dining room, which each evening that week, their homework done, Charlotte and Emily continued to explore.

Charlotte took to reading the books that had gold-edged pages, rather tarnished. They had mostly belonged to Arthur, having such titles as *With Nelson at Trafalgar, With Wellington at Waterloo* or *With Clive in India*, and told of battles, of brave drummer-boys and midshipmen who defied whole armies and navies, so saving the day for everyone. Charlotte was stirred by them, made to feel brave herself or else sometimes very small and cowardly. Arthur, who had become a soldier, must have been very brave, she thought. Most people must be much braver than she, especially boys and men.

Once Mr Chisel Brown left his newspaper in the dining room and Charlotte looked at that instead, at its endless lists of soldiers killed. It made her start to worry about Emily's father, wondering if he would get killed in the war too, wondering what would happen to Emily if he did, Emily having no one now that Clare was gone. But of course there was Bunty's father also out there in France, so many other people's fathers.

Several nights that week Charlotte dreamed, the oddest muddled dreams: rooms at Flintlock Lodge shifting into rooms at Aviary Hall; Grandfather

Elijah appearing with Mr Chisel Brown's moustache; the 'Mark of the Beast' picture containing the faces of people that she knew from every time and place. It was annoying that her sleep should be so confused, because sometimes, by day, she felt peaceful and calm, relieved to be one person all the time, instead of two, even though it was, so worryingly, the wrong person.

On Saturday morning Mr and Mrs Chisel Brown went out for a drive with a friend; Miss Agnes went up to the hospital to read to wounded soldiers; Charlotte and Emily went for a walk with the maid. The weather had been violent for several days, strong winds and gusty rain, the bursts of sunlight in between making colours violent too. But it was calm and fine today, with a softer sun. The wind was so light that when Charlotte held up a wetted finger to find which way it blew she scarcely felt any coldness on her skin. Along the road the remaining leaves were as palely delicate as they would be in spring. But if it had been spring, thought Charlotte, last spring, she would not have been here at all. She found herself hoping desperately she would not be here next spring.

Systematically, deliberately, Emily maddened Ann the maid. She kept stopping to peel leaves from the pavement, plane leaves with many corners that left their damp shapes perfect on the stone. She insisted too, on kicking a pebble wherever they went, stopping to retrieve it from the gutter or from behind the trees. As a result Ann brought them home again almost at once, and retired to her basement, slamming the door.

'Right,' said Emily with satisfaction. 'I know where the ladder's kept.'

It was a long ladder, much longer than they needed, and very heavy. They carried it, panting, from behind a garden shed, breaking leaves and twigs in their manœuvring of it between shrubs and bushes on to the lawn. When the ladder had been propped against the monkey-puzzle tree, its top well above the lowest branches, Charlotte tested carefully to make sure that it was firmly wedged. Then she propped herself up against the old trunk, fingering roughness and scraping bark dust into her finger-nails, while Emily's feet went pounding up the rungs. She could both feel and hear the ladder's shake, but did not want to watch. Just as she had been alarmed to see Emma climb fearlessly, in case she fell, so now it alarmed her to see Emily. She wondered if Clare would have worried too. Emily she realized had not mentioned Clare all this week, and if Charlotte did Emily had pretended not to hear.

'Clare . . . Clare . . . look at me.'

Charlotte craned upwards to discover Emily almost at the top of the tree. 'Mind . . . Oh, mind out . . . Don't go too high.'

'I'm all right. It's easy. It's ripping up here. I can see the river – oh, I can see everything. Why don't you come up too?'

Charlotte looked up doubtfully, wondering why, as she grew older, she seemed to be more afraid of things not less.

'Just come to the top of the ladder,' Emily was shouting. 'That's quite all right, really it is.'

Even to Charlotte ladders were safe, comforting things. Feet, hands gripped tight, moved evenly. Up she went until she was within the bowl that the branches made, hanging down all around, the patterns they formed turning the world to Chinese puzzle shapes. But still she felt quite safe and confident. On up she went. It was trickier here. Though still on the ladder, she had to edge her way round an awkward branch and felt sickened and horrid as she always did, conscious of the height that there was to fall, trying to make herself think about the time when she would be safe again, about Miss Agnes's brother Arthur, who would not have been afraid.

When it was over, she grasped the top rung thankfully and looked up into the tree. She could see Emily's feet so much nearer now, but well above her still, Emily's legs and body tapering up, her face flat because bent to peer down through the branches amid the sun's small dazzle of light. She started to descend the tree towards Charlotte, showering dust and little twigs into her eyes. Charlotte turned her face down and away and found herself looking through a bedroom window almost on a level with her head. She saw a mahogany dressing-table with an oval mirror, and on the wall behind, a framed photograph of a cricket team, men with caps on, standing like clothes pegs, arms folded, legs planted well apart.

Emily looked scraped and breathless, her clothes and legs, just above Charlotte, black with the dust of the tree.

'Gosh, it was easy,' she said. 'Like a ladder, but spikier. I said it would be easy, didn't I?'

'Look.' Charlotte pointed. 'Look, I'm sure that must have been Arthur's room. There's a cricketing photograph.'

Emily bent and peered. 'It must be something to do with Mr Chisel Brown. We can easily find out though. We can ask Ugly Aggie.'

'No, don't let's do that.'

'Why ever not?'

'I just think she mightn't like us asking questions all the time. It seems awfully rude. And perhaps she minds because he's dead.'

'You would say it was rude, but I think she likes us asking. I'll ask her anyway.'

There was a scare then, for they thought they heard wheels, bearing home the Chisel Browns. They scurried down the ladder, Charlotte almost forgetting to fear the awkward place in her greater fear that they should be discovered. This turned out a false alarm, but they had barely returned the ladder to the shed when the grown-ups did return, all three at once, to scold them – but only for being dirty (Mr Chisel Brown, that is, via Miss Agnes Chisel Brown) and not for the more serious offence they would have discovered five minutes earlier when they had been up the tree.

Charlotte and Emily were excited and giggly as they went upstairs again.

'Did you see Ugly Aggie's face?' cried Emily.

'Emily, you mustn't call her that,' said Charlotte feebly. 'She'll hear one day. And besides . . .'

'It's not . . .' said Emily naughtily.

'It's not . . .' said Charlotte more feebly.

'It's not . . .' cried Emily, flopping on her bed. 'It's not Christian.' And they both burst into giggles, growing wilder and wilder, Charlotte, once she had let herself start laughing, finding that she could scarcely stop. But she caught herself, made herself, and tried to make Emily stop too. Clare wouldn't have behaved like that, she told herself severely. 'But then I'm not Clare, I'm not,' she cried inside her head, taking a hairbrush and starting firmly to brush dust and twigs out of her hair.

Much later, in the dining room, Charlotte suddenly said, astonished, 'Emily, you called me Clare when you were up the monkey-puzzle tree.'

'Did I? Don't I always?'

'Only in front of other people. Not always then. You don't call me anything.'

'They'd think it funny, wouldn't they, if they heard me shouting Charlotte at you? Someone might have heard. Anyway,' added Emily after a longish pause, 'anyway, you seem like Clare now.'

'Do I really, though I'm not?'

Emily nodded, but did not look at her. She had the draughts out this evening, making a tower on the table with them, black and white alternately, so that the tower was thickly striped.

'Of course you want Clare back again. I feel awful sometimes being here instead of her. I mean, it must be horrid for you.'

'How can she come? You haven't any ideas how to get her back, have you? Ones that you haven't told me?'

Charlotte had to admit that she had thought of nothing.

'Well then, you see? Will you play draughts with me now, Clare? I bet I'll beat you too.'

Draughts needed a different skill from spillikins, less concentration of fingers or even of eyes than of mind, able to make pictures for itself of moves far on ahead. Emily was much better at this than Charlotte, especially as Charlotte's brain had been made to churn once more round its usual problem: how to get back into her own time. Halfway through their third game, Emily said casually, not looking at Charlotte, 'I did have one idea, actually, to get Clare back I mean. I thought you could creep out of here one night and climb into school by the day-girls' cloakroom. And then you could climb upstairs and go to sleep in that bed.'

It was Charlotte's turn to play. She stared hopelessly at the chequered board. 'But there are people in that room with flu, I couldn't very well turn someone out of bed, could I, to sleep on the floor?'

'You could explain what was happening.'

'And what about the blackout? How could I see my way without any lights?'

'You could go on a moonlit night. Oh, hurry up and play now, it's been your turn for ages.'

Charlotte hurriedly moved the draught nearest her, seeing the mistake at once, for Emily, in triumph, made another king. She was certain to win the third game now, as she had the other two.

'I might have known,' she said, 'you wouldn't want to try. It doesn't matter anyway. One bossy sister's much like another, don't you think? What difference does it make, which one of you is here?'

On their way to church next day, Emily asked Miss Agnes about the room they had seen from the monkey-puzzle tree.

'Oh, that's Arthur's room,' Miss Agnes replied, seeming pleased that they were interested, as Emily had said. 'I used to have the room next door to it, where you and Clare now sleep. Would you like to see it? I haven't time to show you this morning, because of lunch, but perhaps this afternoon . . .'

In the room, its windows tightly closed, lingered some smell that Charlotte had known when she was a little girl, though till now she had quite forgotten it: a faint, sour, man's smell. She remembered it in her father's cupboard among his best silk handkerchiefs, where she used to bury her face because they felt so comforting and cool, like water, on her skin.

Arthur Chisel Brown had a cupboard like her father's, its narrow compartments still full of collars, handkerchiefs and socks, while beneath them sat a row of polished shoes and a pair of well-whitened cricket boots.

'We've left everything, you see, just as it always was,' explained Miss Agnes. 'Even the bed's made up. Mrs Chisel Brown would have nothing changed. I dust in here myself each day. If Arthur came home tomorrow we should be ready for him. Look, there are even biscuits in his tin.'

What Charlotte and Emily both liked best was something that hung upon the wall: a drum, a full-sized soldier's drum, not a toy at all, its sides striped diagonally in green and gold, its skin kept taut by narrow cords. Charlotte rolled her fingers across it experimentally, finding it almost furry to touch, not smooth as she had expected. Then Emily tapped lightly with her fingers' ends. The noise was surprising for such moderate strokes, still thrumming and rolling a little when she had taken her hands away.

'Sssssssh . . . carefully, Emily,' said Miss Agnes, turning round in alarm. 'Mr and Mrs Chisel Brown may hear if you do that.'

'Why?' asked Emily. 'Wouldn't they have wanted us to come in here?'

'Of course I should not have brought you, if it meant displeasing them,' Miss Agnes insisted hurriedly, though pink spots had become noticeable in her cheeks.

'*Why* did he have a drum?' asked Emily.

'It's a soldier's drum. He was interested in soldiers as you know.'

'He must have wanted to be a soldier. He was lucky to become a soldier when he grew up, wasn't he?' said Emily.

'He didn't become a soldier till the war though, dear. Mr and Mrs Chisel Brown wouldn't hear of it earlier. They said it wasn't safe enough. I wonder if you are both too young, Clare and Emily, to remember those posters early in the war – Lord Kitchener pointing with such a fierce, dutiful look, while underneath it said, "Your Country Needs You". They moved dear Arthur so, that he said to me one day, "Aggie, I *must* join up though it will upset dear Mother dreadfully." '

'And did he like it, fighting in the war?' asked Emily.

'I expect so, dear.' But after a minute Miss Agnes added less brightly, 'It wasn't like his books, he said, like the battles he fought there. He said it was so muddy, I would not believe.

'Look, dears,' she said, moving hurriedly to one of the photographs that hung all round the walls, of cricket, football and tennis teams. 'Look, there he is. That's my brother Arthur.'

The photograph was dated 1913, the year before the war began, but the photographer might have been the enemy already, the way Arthur glared at him. He was a small man, smaller than most in his team, with thick eyebrows like Miss Agnes's, and the largest moustache in the group by far. He wore a striped cap, and what looked to be the same striped blazer as hung in the cupboard now.

'Goodness, he did look fierce,' said Emily.

'He wasn't fierce really, dear, he wasn't fierce at all, though sometimes he pretended to be.'

One evening in the back of the toy cupboard Charlotte found an old exercise book and asked Miss Agnes if she might look through it. It had a story in it, some bits of other stories, also drawings, rather brown and faded-looking now, because done by Arthur when a boy. The story had only four chapters, and it was easy to see where Arthur had found his plot, for it was about a brave drummer-boy, whom everyone called a coward at first till he saved them in battle and died nobly. The other stories were about battles too, about drummer-boys or midshipmen. The drawings were mostly of soldiers or guns, but there were some odd-looking animals, horses, elephants and lions. Charlotte found it hard to associate such things with the baleful-looking man in the cricketing photograph.

That evening and most evenings now, Miss Agnes came and played games with them, card games, Old Maid, Rummy or Demon Patience.

She also talked, usually it seemed of her brother Arthur. Whenever she had excuse to, she talked about him briskly, eagerly, excitedly and sometimes defiantly; how handsome he was, how clever and bright, how naughty, but how brave.

Miss Agnes, Charlotte thought, was a bit like Clare and a bit like herself, with a naughty younger brother instead of sister to keep in order. Suppose she were to change places with her, become Arthur's elder sister instead of Emma's or Emily's? It was an easy thought, Charlotte decided, because quite impossible.

# CHAPTER FOUR

NIGHT after night, Charlotte lay in bed with her eyes open to the dark, thinking up wild and yet wilder schemes for getting herself back to school by night to sleep in the bed with wheels. The trouble was that, as Charlotte, she was not someone who did wild things, except in extraordinary circumstances; and as Clare, she could not imagine herself doing anything wild at all, certainly nothing so wild as going out at night. But she reckoned in this without Emily.

That week, Emily became interested in the night sky. Each evening when their light was out she craned her head from the window to see, complaining the first night because the moon was so small, and even more disappointed the next four nights because the cloud was too thick for her to see the moon at all. On Friday night she said with satisfaction, 'Just as I thought. The moon's coming up now, and it's going to be full. We'll be able to see quite easily.'

'Be able to see what?' asked Charlotte, still unsuspecting, which she realized a moment afterwards was stupid of her.

'See to get to the school, of course. I thought tonight you could try to sleep in that bed.'

Charlotte was horrified. 'Emily,' she said sternly, 'Emily, I told you it wouldn't be any use doing that. Supposing we're caught. We'd probably be expelled and that wouldn't help at all.'

'Well, I'm going anyway.'

'But whatever's the point of your going alone?' Charlotte did not add that Emily could not get Clare back by herself, because it seemed unkind.

Emily said, 'I know I can't get Clare back by going, but I'm going anyway. If I'm caught I'll get into trouble for nothing. If you come, at least there's some point in it.'

Charlotte saw the logic in this, so gave in reluctantly. But whether the decision arose from her greater adventurousness as Charlotte, or from her special sense of responsibility towards Emily as Clare, she could not tell.

'How are we going to get in if we do get to the school?' she asked.

'I've opened the window in the day-girls' cloakroom every day this week. At least, I only turned the catch, so the window still looks quite shut. Don't you remember, I've kept on forgetting things and going back when everyone else has gone?'

Emily woke Charlotte some time before midnight. They dressed themselves hurriedly in the dark, and then crept downstairs to the kitchen; the opening of the basement door less likely to be heard, they thought, than the opening of the front door one stair-flight higher. Charlotte was in terror of being caught; horrified by every creak the stairs made; appalled by all the kitchen sounds – clickings, rustlings, the sudden urgent crackle of the kitchen stove, the ponderous metal ticking of the clock. The two clock weights hung in shadow, but the pendulum on its narrow rod swung past them from light to light, from one moonlit square to another reflecting silver and not its usual warm brass wink.

The door opposite had been fastened by all imaginable means. There was a bar to be lifted off, a chain to be unhooked, bolts at the top and bottom to be heaved back with difficulty, and finally a key to be turned. The noise this made drowned all the other sounds that had seemed so noisy earlier, was so loud that it even worried Emily, but Charlotte by now was numbed enough by fear to be almost beyond worrying, pelting blindly up the basement steps, across the gravel, and out at last into the freedom of the road.

It was cold tonight, a little frosty – both were glad of their thick school coats. Charlotte wore gloves too, but Emily had flung hers down unthinkingly the night before, and had been unable find them in the dark. When she complained that her hands were cold Charlotte handed over her own gloves, and huddled her hands in her pockets.

The streets looked strange, lightless, save for the moon, which laid not a glitter or a shine, but a texture, a kind of silver fuzz on everything, eliminating roughness and curves. Even the blackest shadows seemed muffled, their blackness of velvet rather than of polish or paint. As they went farther from the house, still meeting no one, Charlotte's guilty fear started to fade away, and she felt excited, almost exhilarated by this empty world. These streets were the ones that they walked along each morning and afternoon and yet quite different, for they had their own separate, breathing life that the country always has, but that towns do not by day. Even her footsteps did not seem to belong to her. The night seized and transformed them, just as it transformed the greenhouses they passed from useful places for growing things into cold night palaces.

Once they thought they heard footsteps and dived behind some convenient trees. But the footsteps, if that was what they were, had died away at once and they emerged giggling at each other with the nicest sense of conspiracy, Charlotte as much as Emily. Not long afterwards, much too soon for Charlotte, they reached the spiked school gates. They were firmly closed. The moonlight had drained all the colour left in their faded Union Jacks. Behind them, to one side of the drive, the lodge stood, but its lodge-keeper they knew to be quite old and deaf, which tonight was just as well.

Charlotte began to climb first, her nervousness returning. The gates, though high, were well ornamented, the loops and curves offering footholds for smallish feet. She put both their coats to pad the topmost spikes and used for a final step the wooden board that announced the name of the school. From there she lowered herself cautiously, but Emily scrambled like a monkey after her, clinging with hands and feet till barely halfway down, then launching out to jump the rest.

'Bother,' she said from the ground. 'Bother, I forgot the coats,' and climbed up again to fetch them. She was still poised, trying to free one from the spikes, when they heard more footsteps, this time unmistakably drawing nearer. Emily wrenched at the cloth. tearing it a little, the sound quite clear in the frosty air, and then threw herself violently from the gate. As she picked herself up, Charlotte grabbed the coats and they both ran furiously over the grass into the deeper shadow of the wall. Behind them the flags still shivered, the gates still shook from Emily's jump.

It was two policewomen who came, walking rhythmically. They shook the gates almost before looking at them, so disguising any movement that might have remained for them to see. They peered through and when they had shaken the gates again still harder they passed on, their footsteps fading evenly. But it was minutes still before Charlotte and Emily dared to move again, to drag on their coats and set off surreptitiously over the grass.

'Gosh,' said Emily. 'Gosh, we'd have been for it if they'd seen us.'

Charlotte's elation had suddenly disappeared. She was terrified again, wishing only that she was safe in bed. Every upright tree and bush held in its shadow a Miss Bite, a Nurse Gregory or a Miss Wilkin, ready to jump out at them. Each cabbage in the vegetable bed, each leafy potato plant had its own shadow and watchfulness. She began to hope that someone would have discovered the window-latch undone, and so shut the window properly again. They would have to go back home then, to Flintlock Lodge, without more dangerous ventures.

But Emily whispered, as if thought-reading, 'If it isn't open, I think we should break it to get in. It would be silly to come all this way for nothing.'

It's all very well for you, Charlotte allowed herself to think, though not to say. It's not you, Emily, that's got to climb in, do the really dangerous part.

The window was in the corner of an arcade, and so not overlooked by any bedrooms. It was round, like a large porthole, and stood just out of reach of

Charlotte's hands, so that she had to lift Emily awkwardly to test whether it remained unlatched, making her arms feel as though they would break.

'It's all right,' said Emily at long last. 'It's all right. It's open, we won't have to break in after all.'

It was her turn to heave Charlotte now. Charlotte's feet scrabbled against the wall, her hands clutched at the slippery window ledge, her arms somehow pulled her high enough for her to get first one elbow, then the other across the sill, and so to haul herself through at last, grunting furiously and kicking up her feet behind.

Then awkwardly she turned and knelt on the draining-board to look down at Emily.

'Well done, Clare, oh, well done,' she was saying in her whisper that was louder than most people's shouts. Charlotte felt triumphant too, for all her fright, for all the burning of her scraped knees and elbows and the dent in her stomach made by the window-frame.

'Hey, Clare,' Emily was hissing. 'Hey, Clare. What if you do get into that bed again? You won't come back, but I can't wait here till the morning.'

If this difficulty had crossed Charlotte's mind it had not really entered it or concerned it, for she had never believed they would get as far as this.

'Well, if I don't come for ages and ages, well . . . you'd better just go home,' she whispered lamely, wondering what Clare would do when and if she woke, for she would have no idea at all where to go to find Emily.

Outside the cloakroom with its carbolic reek the corridors were dark and stale-smelling, quenching any triumph that was left in Charlotte. Moonlight edged in a little here and there, and she had to fumble along the wall, farther and farther away from Emily and safety. The stairs creaked and were still more dangerous; at the top of them the corridor was lit, the light, though dim, bright-seeming to Charlotte's unaccustomed eyes. The walls were drab with their shiny brown paint and bare, without any place to hide, the dents made by the doorways too shallow to give cover.

Day-girls were forbidden to go upstairs. Charlotte had not been there at all since she and Emily left for Flintlock Lodge, and so she saw the corridor at first quite newly, her eyes taking time to fit it to the expected pattern. She stood for a long time, because numbed by the closeness and nostalgia of what she saw, feeling both so near to her proper self and existence and yet so far away.

Then, when she did remember what she had come to do, it seemed so dangerous that she considered turning back at once, telling Emily that there was someone in the bed already who refused to move, without venturing to find out if it was so. But she did not think this honourable, did not think that she could lie convincingly. Besides, the door of the room was so tantalizingly near, just a few yards down the corridor and across. There was no sound except the tiny sounds she made herself, breathing and gripping the stair rail. No one came. She took a deeper breath, made a tiptoed dive for the door, pushed it open, fell inside, closing the door behind her silently, in her haste more by luck than skill.

The blackout covered the window. The room was like a cave. A nightlight burnt by the very bed that she had come to find, a little cave of light within the larger cave of darkness. It looked the reverse of moonlight, warm and mobile, rounding things, making shadows move. In all the other beds forms lay still, asleep. But in that bed, the one with little wheels, someone propped up on pillows stirred and coughed and moaned.

Charlotte took this in; then footsteps sounded. They were like delayed echoes of her own at first, but grew quickly louder and more purposeful. Click, click, click, they went, slap, slap, slap, daytime footsteps seemingly, not muted in respect for the night, pausing at last outside this very door. The handle turned smartly. Something rattled against glass. In came a tray, someone carrying it. She looked, as always, sharp-edged, as if night was as normal as the day to her, sounded like a sailing boat in a small wind, shoes creaking, stiff apron flapping, the liquid slapping in a small glass. It was Nurse Gregory.

# CHAPTER FIVE

A T the first sound of footsteps Charlotte had flung herself into the only hiding place she could see, the small space between the big white cupboard and the end wall. Since she and Emily had left, a chest-of-drawers had been moved in just behind the door. This helped to shelter her if she crouched right down, as did the shadow of the door, which Nurse Gregory had left open, lightening a little the rest of the room but dimming the corner more.

For the moment Nurse Gregory's back was turned. She was briskly telling her patient to sit up, and after that Charlotte heard a kind of spluttering, as if the girl had not expected medicine to reach her mouth so fast.

Terror made Charlotte feel remote, like an audience in a theatre. Crouched right down she could not see much that was happening in the area of light, but she could see the shadows bumping and jumbling on the ceiling. Nurse Gregory's shadow was elongated, huge, stretching right across the room. The shadow that her arms made rose and fell from the larger one, like claws or branches.

Suddenly Nurse Gregory turned away and advanced towards the door. For one horrible moment she paused again. Charlotte wanted to leap up, jump out and explain herself at once before being dragged forth ignominiously. It was only the knowledge that she could not explain anything convincingly that prevented her. In any case, Nurse Gregory merely tucked in a trailing blanket and moved on with an intolerably loud rustle and hammerblows of feet until at last, loudly, she closed the door behind her.

In other beds, figures began to stir. The girl in the bed with the wheels shook her head from side to side and cried, 'No, no,' as if, too late, to Nurse Gregory. Charlotte moved her feet, which had been cramped unbearably, to find them riddled at once with pins and needles. After a while she stood up. She was trembling all over. She did not know how she would dare leave the room again, let alone the school.

She strained her ears, listening, thinking all the time that she heard the sound of Nurse Gregory's feet. But she heard only the stirrings in the room.

She grabbed enough courage at last to make what seemed the most difficult move in all her life, and crept to the door, opening it the smallest crack. She saw nothing, heard no sound. Hesitating still, she glanced back into the room, to see eyes open suddenly in the nearest bed. A face looked at her in astonishment – the face of Bunty's friend Ruth.

Charlotte ran, not even shutting the door behind her, out into the empty passage, and a moment later into the black darkness of the stairhead. She did not even look back to see if anyone was coming. Her heart felt like a rod in a machine, going strong and hard, thump, thump, thump.

How she got downstairs and out of the window she could afterwards scarcely remember. She found Emily indignant, and seemingly a little disappointed at seeing her.

'You were ages,' she said. 'I'm as cold as ice. I was jolly nearly going home too. I thought you must have got into the bed, you were such ages and ages.'

'Was I?' said Charlotte, astonished. 'It didn't seem like any time to me.'

When they looked back after climbing the school gates, the moon was already much lower, but two brilliant tubes of light swung about the sky, advancing, crossing each other, like a dance.

'Searchlights,' said Emily. 'To catch aeroplanes, you know. Gosh, suppose there's an air raid now, that would finish us, wouldn't it?' But she sounded quite happy about it. Charlotte was too dazed to care. She must have been mad to do what she had just been doing. It seemed impossible, an uncomfortable dream.

On Monday, when they went back to school again, there were still footmarks up the wall by the day-girls' cloakroom. No one seemed to notice them except Charlotte and Emily, but then no one else would have expected to find them there.

The day after the expedition Emily had been morose, silent. Charlotte, exhausted, thought that probably she was just tired too. By today, though, she was normal again and cheerful, not morose at all. She had not mentioned their failure the whole weekend, nor did she mention it now.

*

Clare had always been a kind of skin about her, Charlotte thought, containing what she did and said and was; but the skin had thickened imperceptibly the longer she stayed in the past. After the night-time expedition it began to thicken more rapidly than ever, pressing that part of her which still thought of itself as Charlotte tighter and smaller, until it lay deep down in her, like a small stone inside a large plum.

One day, recognizing a certain picture on the walls of Miss Bite's room, of two women at a spinning-wheel, with flowing robes and with faces smooth as angels' faces, she could not think at all where she had seen it before, or when – in the present or in the past. As her memory struggled to disentangle its two lives, she caught herself wondering even if it was something to do with Aunt Dolly's house, then remembered, immediately and with a shock, that she had never been to Aunt Dolly's house nor seen Aunt Dolly.

'I'm going to have six children when I grow up,' said Bunty that day. 'How many are you going to have, Emily? How many are you going to have, Elsie Brand?'

Emily said nothing. Elsie merely grunted.

'I expect Elsie will have ten, won't you, Elsie?' cried someone else. 'And they'll all eat sausage and be called things like Fritz and Gretel.'

Everybody giggled, except for Charlotte, who cried indignantly, but hopelessly, 'Don't be so horrid. They'll have ordinary names like John and Susan, won't they, Elsie?'

But Elsie did not reply. She looked as blankly, dully, at Charlotte as at the rest.

'How many children will you have, Emily?' asked Bunty, once again.

'I'm not going to have any children.'

'Aren't you going to get married then?'

'Oh yes, I might get married. But I shan't have children all the same.'

'Emily, why ever not?' the voice sounded almost shocked. 'Everyone has children when they get married.'

'Not everyone does. And I won't. I won't.'

'But why ever not?'

'Because, because, it's so awful for them, I mean it would be if I died and they had nowhere to live and they had to go round and stay with all sorts of people who didn't want to have them.'

'Why?' said Bunty, quite gently for her. 'Why, Emily, is that what happens to you and Clare?'

Emily did not reply. Bunty looked at Charlotte and persisted.

'Is that what happens to you and Emily, Clare?'

Emily usually answered all such questions, even those addressed to Charlotte, but still she answered nothing at all. Everyone except Emily was looking at Charlotte now. She blushed and cleared her throat and scratched at the desk with her fingernail, but the odd thing was that once she had started to speak she knew it all so well that she might have been talking about Emily and herself and not about Emily and Clare.

'We do stay with a lot of people, I suppose. Aunt Dolly likes having us, but she's ill sometimes, so we have to go away. But of course people don't really mind having us, it's very kind of them – isn't it, Emily – Aunt Dolly always says.'

It was after this that Charlotte began to dream she was fighting to stay as Charlotte; and one night woke from such a dream, struggling, even crying a little. When she was calm again she did not feel sleepy at all, so she lay carefully and deliberately making herself remember Aviary Hall; object by object; room by room. Also she made herself remember things that had happened to her as Charlotte, but it was alarming how the details seemed to slip away from her. Even when she tried to conjure up her sister Emma's face she kept on seeing Emily's.

Then she found herself thinking about Agnes's brother Arthur, instead, about his room and all the things Miss Agnes had told her about him. She did not try to stop these thoughts because they seemed safe and comfortable, making a third and separate existence in which neither as Charlotte nor Clare was she involved.

When she fell asleep again she dreamed about Arthur, both the boy in the tinted photograph and the man with the big moustache. He climbed the monkey-puzzle tree and banged his soldier's drum. He wore a soldier's uniform and sat in a muddy field, and then suddenly he was setting out his soldiers on the dining-room table and she sat beside him, watching him as if she were his sister Agnes too, not Charlotte, not Clare.

# CHAPTER SIX

ONE Wednesday afternoon the school had a half-holiday and Miss Agnes took Charlotte and Emily across the river to do some shopping. They had to go by the station to fetch a parcel, and found a small crowd gathered outside and all along the road lines of white ambulances, each having a red cross painted on its side.

'The hospital train's just in now, lady,' the woman at the ticket office said. 'You'll have to wait a bit till we let the wounded through.'

Miss Agnes tried to hurry away with Charlotte and Emily, but the crowd had thickened so much that they found themselves wedged in front of it, beneath the station's shabby canopy and fringe.

Charlotte was used to all the marks of war; the shabbiness of things, bad food, shop queues, posters about the war effort, people with worried faces, people dressed in black. She was used to seeing the wounded men from the hospital wearing their bright blue uniforms and bright red ties, the colours, she thought, if not the clothes of Arthur's soldiers. Such things did not disturb her and the war seemed quite remote. But this disturbed her, this grotesque kind of circus that came now. It did not seem remote at all, nor did it fit into her vague ideas of war gained from those books of Arthur's she had read, full of flags and glory and brave drummer-boys. How could you dare to become a soldier, knowing that you might end like this? There were men like clowns, with white heads, white arms, white legs; men with crutches, slings and bloodied bandages and all so distressingly like men you would expect to see walking down the street, two-armed, two-legged, in hats instead of bandages and suits of black not battered khaki. Some came on stretchers borne by whole and ordinary men, some hobbled and leaned on whole ordinary arms. Most had mud dried thick across their clothes and all came from the dark station's mouth, with the spewings of trains behind, the clankings, thumpings, grindings, the sounds like great devils taking in breaths and blowing them out again.

The war however was clearly coming to an end. At school the children were elated and excited. To hear them talk it might have been a school match won, rather than a war. But their excitement was not reflected among the staff, and at Flintlock Lodge the subject was scarcely mentioned now, mainly because it made Mr Chisel Brown so angry, especially at breakfast when he first read his newspaper. No one was meant to disturb him then by talk of any kind. A dumb waiter, a round tray on a pedestal, stood in the centre of the table with all the food on it. You had to spin the tray gently if you wanted something, milk or margarine or marmalade, till the jug or dish stood opposite your place. But one morning, Mr Chisel Brown's newspaper so angered him by talk of peace that he set the tray spinning like a top. Toast shot out at angles, salt cellar jumbled with pepper pot, marmalade was flung on to the margarine. Emily was delighted, giggling openly; so, more discreetly, was Charlotte.

'Conchies, huns, ought to be hanged,' muttered scarlet Mr Chisel Brown, whether at them or the

newspaper it was hard to tell. But Mrs Chisel
Brown continued eating toast, as if she had not
noticed what had happened, putting the slice that
had fallen nearest her on her own plate.

Emily these days was a friend of Ann the maid.
At least, she spent a lot of time talking to her, or
rather bickering, if amicably. That morning she
rushed from Ann to Charlotte in a state of great
excitement.

'Ann says the Chisel Browns are going to have
a seance,' she said.

'A what?' asked Charlotte.

'A seance. A spiritualist seance. Don't you know
what that is? I know, Ann told me. It's to make
dead people talk to you. There's a lady who
comes, called a medium, and everyone sits round
her and the dead person speaks through her and
gives messages to people still alive and answers
questions too.'

'But how can someone answer questions who's
dead?'

'Ann says spiritualists don't say people are dead
they say they've passed over to the other side. She
says the mediums are sort of telephones sending
messages on. It's a sort of magic they've got, like
fortune-tellers, you know, who can tell what's

going to happen in the future. Ann went to a seance once, to speak to her young man who was killed in the war. She says she really did speak to him, he said all sorts of things no one would have known except him. When the Chisel Browns have their seance she's going to look through the keyhole and see what happens, and I want to too.'

'I should have thought it would be difficult for two people to look through a keyhole at once, and I think perhaps it isn't a very nice thing to do.'

'Of course I'm not going to look through the keyhole. That's something only servants do. I'm going to hide in the bay window. It would be quite safe there with the curtains drawn across.'

'I don't see that it's different from looking through the keyhole myself.'

'Oh, don't be such a prig, Clare. Don't you want to see what happens?'

'I don't believe anything *will* happen.'

'Well, Ann does, and the Chisel Browns and Aggie, and they're all grown-up people. They wouldn't have asked the medium to come if they didn't believe in it.'

'Who do they want to speak to anyway?'

'Why, Arthur of course, silly,' said Emily. 'Don't you want to hear what he says? I thought you would, the amount old Aggie talks about him. In fact, I'm a bit sick of him myself, I bet he wasn't really so handsome and brave and clever at all. Ann says he wasn't like that a bit.'

'Of course he was brave,' said Charlotte. 'Of course he was brave. He was a soldier, wasn't he?'

At school, since Ruth was still in bed with flu, Emily went around with Bunty all the time. This had begun to happen even before Ruth went. She and Charlotte had been left more often than not to keep each other company. Now Charlotte was left on her own. All the same she dreaded Ruth's return, for what would Ruth have to say about seeing her that night? She half expected that Ruth would have let it out to someone already – to Nurse Gregory perhaps; had expected to be summoned for questioning by Nurse Gregory or by Miss Bite herself. But she never had been. She had not told Emily about being seen and did not now tell any of her fears.

One morning in break time someone gave Charlotte a letter for Clare and Emily from their father in France. They were all supposed to be out in the garden, as in every kind of weather, but though Charlotte found Olive, Peggy, Margaret,

Dorothy, Susan, Joan – almost everyone, in fact, she found no sign of Emily or Bunty.

'I think they went that way,' someone pointed towards an end of the garden Charlotte had never explored, for it was out of bounds. In her own time it had led into the Japanese gardens. She wondered if it did now, and a rather nostalgic curiosity took her round the edges of the bushes and into the forbidden territory at a moment she was sure no one would see her go.

It did not look so different from when she had seen it in her own time, except that then it had been September and now it was November, and a dripping, dismal, blackish day at that.

Charlotte pushed her way uncomfortably through the wet bushes with their whippy twigs, to find the lake, the bridge, the curiously shaped trees, most still with leaves on them, but drooping now and seeming to absorb the dank and dismal light as much as they had absorbed the glow of sun before. The garden was more overgrown if anything, the black lake choked by leaves and water-lily plants and bent brown reeds. Only the bridge looked newer, missing no slats or rails, its paintwork barely flaked at all. It was a dark-pink dreary paint, which had been prettier faded, Charlotte thought.

On the bridge, staring down at the water and giggling uncontrollably were Emily and Bunty. They did not notice Charlotte, who stood close among the bushes, still thinking about the last person she had seen standing on the bridge: Sarah Reynolds.

She had not thought about Sarah for weeks; but could see her in her mind as clearly as if she'd met her yesterday, tall and fair, with that curious walk like ropes slackening in her at each step, then tightening again; with her slow, incurious smile; Sarah Reynolds whom she had thought might be called Moby, and so be the daughter of either Clare or Emily.

Charlotte shook herself at this, and made the bushes shake too. Bunty and Emily looked round at once, and stopped giggling when they saw Charlotte.

'What are you doing here?' asked Emily rudely.

'What are *you* doing here? And what are you giggling about?'

'We're getting away from bossy older sisters, if you must know.'

'It's out of bounds here.'

'Well, you're out of bounds too, aren't you?'

'We like it here, nobody interferes with us – we mean anybody, prefects and people, not just you,' explained Bunty less hostile than Emily.

'Well, *usually* nobody interferes with us,' said Emily pointedly.

'If you're going to be rude,' said Charlotte, 'I won't tell you why I came.' But she was too kind to continue. 'It's a letter, actually, from Daddy,' she added self-consciously.

'Oh, you lucky thing! It's time I had a letter from my father,' Bunty cried.

Emily had jumped from the bridge and snatched the letter from Charlotte without saying a word. She tore it open anxiously as she always did but then laughed several times in the reading of it.

'Aren't you going to let Clare read it too?' asked Bunty curiously.

They hurried back afterwards but found they'd missed the bell for the end of break, and that almost everyone else had already gone indoors, except for the two prefects in charge, one of whom saw the three coming from where they never should have gone. Bunty had the worst scolding for she had slipped beside the lake, and was particularly muddy and wet.

They had to sit in the big classroom, doing preparation in charge of Miss Wilkin, whose fiancé had been killed at the front the week before.

Though as neat as ever, she looked bedraggled somehow, a little shrunk, her clothes not quite so tight on her as before. Certainly she was not jolly any more. She had pen and paper but did not write; she twisted her ring continually, but did not look at it. No one now tried to play her up, yet it was hard not to take the slightest advantage of her lack of interest in what they did, and Bunty and Emily sat drawing in ink on the backs of their hands, comparing the results with appreciative giggles. They ignored Charlotte's occasional frowns. On Charlotte's other side sat Elsie Brand, who seemed more silent than ever these days, and still took no notice of efforts to be nice to her, though Charlotte tried her hardest to be nice. It worried her that anyone could look as miserable as Elsie did.

Bunty and Emily began to draw on each other's hands. Emily drew a fine, fat pig on Bunty's, dressed in school uniform. She wrote a *B* for Bunty underneath, but Bunty snatched the pen, and had just written *Elsie Brand* instead, when a prefect came into the room and whispered to Miss Wilkin.

'Bunty, Miss Bite wants to see you. Will you go at once?' Miss Wilkin called aloud, in her new, flat, unhappy voice.

'That meanie prefect,' Bunty hissed to Emily. 'I bet she told about us being out of bounds.' She was squeezing between the desks, meanwhile, watched by the prefect with a grave, unmoving face; disapproving, Charlotte thought.

'I wonder why they didn't make us go to see her too,' Emily whispered to Charlotte as the door closed behind the tall prefect and shorter, rounder Bunty.

Emily went on drawing by herself, patterns instead of figures, stars and swirls and dashes, wholly absorbed by what she did. Bunty did not return. Much later, Miss Bite came with her slow, deliberate walk, bent forward, one hand behind her back, placing every foot as a chicken does, as if to scratch at dust. She went first to Miss Wilkin and spoke to her quietly. Miss Wilkin nodded but her head sank farther and farther down and she looked at no one. Miss Bite looked straight towards the class.

'May I have your attention, please, girls?' she asked, as if they had not all secretly been watching and listening to her since she entered the room, wondering who or what she wanted.

'I am afraid I have to tell you, girls,' she said, 'that Marjorie's father has been killed in France.'

(Marjorie? Marjorie? thought Charlotte, before realizing with a horrid jump that Bunty was Marjorie). 'She will not therefore be joining you for the rest of the day, but when she returns tomorrow, I know I need not ask you to be especially kind. Marjorie has asked if Emily Moby may spend part of the afternoon with her, and I have agreed to that request.'

The rest of the class became subdued at this. No one looked at anyone else and talk was hushed. One or two people even cried. Charlotte did not cry, but could not get out of her mind the sight of Bunty's giggling face as she went off to be told such news.

Suppose next time it was Emily's father. At least, unlike Emily, Bunty had mother, brother and sisters left to her. It occurred to Charlotte to wonder how she herself could pretend to show grief for someone she did not know, had never seen, although he was supposed to be her father. But she was ashamed of having such a selfish thought. And of course she knew she would be upset on behalf of Emily.

It happened that just before lunch, Miss Bite sent her to the staffroom with a message, and Charlotte almost bumped into Bunty coming out of Miss

Bite's room nearby. Her eyes were red and she was not looking at anyone, though she gave a sort of half smile at Charlotte. Charlotte half smiled back, as embarrassed as most people are at someone else's sorrow, not wanting accidentally to make Bunty still more sorrowful. Looking down, she caught sight of Bunty's hand, which still showed a faint picture of a pig in school uniform labelled Elsie Brand.

All the rest of that day, a name went on nibbling in Charlotte's head; not Bunty though, nor Elsie Brand; the name of Sarah Reynolds. And it came to her at last, when lying in bed, that a grown-up, married Emily or a grown-up, married Clare would not be called Moby. They would be Smith, Jones, anything, even Reynolds, because women when they married changed their names. Which meant, of course, that one of them, grown up, might be Sarah's mother after all. When she had considered a little more, Charlotte scarcely doubted it, for nothing else explained the things Sarah had said to her.

She wondered which of them: Emily or Clare. She was inclined to think it Clare. Clare sounded more motherly, indeed Charlotte could not imagine Emily as a mother at all. She had said so firmly that she was never going to have children of her own; and that Emily did not easily change her mind, Charlotte knew quite well.

But then, suppose she and Clare remained for good in each other's times, as often seemed likely now? That would mean, thought Charlotte with a horrid lurch, that would mean she herself might grow up to be Sarah Reynold's mother.

# CHAPTER SEVEN

A FTER the news of Bunty's father, Emily became increasingly quiet and withdrawn. She had always tended to be in trouble at school. No one made allowances for her being younger than anyone else, and all her work came back scrawled across with pencil, blue or red, and with words such as 'poor' or 'ill-done' written underneath; for which she was given detentions or sometimes even conduct marks. She had not seemed to mind too much before; had let Charlotte help her sometimes with the work, in fact usually begged her to. Now she still did not say that she minded, but looked as if she did, and would not let Charlotte help at all. Her homework done, she sat playing endless solitary games – of patience or spillikins or draughts. She spent hours arranging the draughts in towers or patterns or trying to balance them round the edges of their box. Once when Miss Agnes did not come she spent half the evening pulling horse-hairs out of the dining-room chairs and arranging them in rows along the table, and the other half scraping dirt with her nails from round the little brass studs that held the leather down.

Next day, Charlotte found a solitaire board and the marbles to fit into its rounded holes. From then on Emily played with that incessantly. She even took it up to bed with her, sat hunched over the board, moving one marble across another till it was time to put out the light.

With Emily like this, Charlotte was quite glad sometimes to have Miss Agnes to talk to, but she too, for some reason, seemed different just now, especially awkward and uncertain. Sometimes when talking of Arthur she would change the subject abruptly to something else. Charlotte wondered if she would mention the seance, but she did not – at least not until the Friday night. Miss Agnes seemed more nervous and edgy then ever then, knocking things over with her elbow, picking them up quickly and putting them down again, starting to say something and not finishing.

Two red patches came to her cheeks, both very firm and bright.

'Did you hear of the seance?' she whispered abruptly. 'Did you hear we were having a seance? Do you know what a seance is, Clare?'

'A little bit, I think.'

'We have a medium coming, a very wonderful lady, I believe, we hope through her to get in touch with dear Arthur. At least, Mrs Chisel Brown . . . I'm not so sure myself . . .' She was looking away from Charlotte, twiddling a white draught between her fingers, round and round. 'But dear Mother was so keen to have it, you know, she thinks of dear Arthur all the time, she was so very fond of him. A friend told us of this medium-lady and she wished to have her here. All those photographs, you know, on her table, they are all of my brother Arthur and she won't let anyone touch them except herself.'

Emily was listening. Without turning her head, Charlotte could see her look up from the solitaire board. But she said nothing at all.

'We are having,' Miss Agnes continued, 'we are having this seance tomorrow.'

In spite of what she had said to Emily before about the seance, Charlotte found herself curious to know what would happen and ready to hide in the window bay, deceitful as that seemed. She was curious about Arthur, having heard so much about him. She wanted to hear what he might say if he did say anything. She went to bed thinking of all she knew of him.

Thus she dreamed about Arthur, not for the first time. She dreamed she stood below the picture, 'The Mark of the Beast', and there were soldiers all round her in red uniforms, stiff as toys, but tall as men. There were dolls too, like Miss Agnes's doll, tall as the soldiers; and when she looked down she was wearing the same kind of clothes as they wore, with boots and a hat and sash behind.

She dreamed she heard a drum beating, and never knew afterwards whether this was a dream or real. Thrum, thrum, thrum, it went reaching into all parts of her head. It might even have come from inside her head. And she thought she heard someone laughing and someone else crying. Then, without seeming to move she found herself standing beside a boy who beat the drum. Its gold and green stripes were bright, its soft top vibrated, it sounded not only like a drum, but also like a roaring aeroplane, and it made lights as well as sounds, beams like searchlights dazzling at every stroke. She was begging the boy to stop. 'Oh, please, Arthur, please, you'll wake everyone up, Papa will hear you, oh, please.'

The boy wore bandages on his head under a cricketer's hat and he laughed and went on beating the drum. 'Why shouldn't I?' he asked, making the drum go thrum, roll like an aeroplane, the sound growing against her head. And she was Miss Agnes in the short humped skirt that the doll had worn, the feather of the doll's hat tickling on her cheek. She began crying bitterly, could not stop, and so at last woke up.

It was silent, also darkish. Yet there was light too. At first, so sleepy, her eyes barely open, Charlotte had merely an impression of it, of a dazzling, or more, perhaps, a shine, but when she opened her eyes properly at last she found it the reflection of light on glass. The glass must have been on the picture 'The Mark of the Beast'; the light certainly was moonlight.

Yet it was odd. There was a difference somewhere. Something in the room had changed. Charlotte lay quite still, with her eyes open, and sensed that, not knowing why or by which sense – sight, smell, hearing. After a moment she turned her head slowly towards Emily's bed and felt the difference still more strongly, yet as intangibly. Moonlight fell on the end of the bed, bleaching all colour from the dark red counterpane. Charlotte turned her head away at once – and as quickly wanted to look back again, to reassure herself that nothing was different after all. And yet she could not, would not look. The simple turning of her head seemed to need as much effort, as much resolve, as a dive into water or a climb up a long wall. She stared at the ceiling instead, which looked blank and ordinary enough.

She dragged at her head, dragged it round at last. But she was not then reassured at all. She sat up quickly, trembling violently, for the bed was flat, the counterpane smooth. There was no Emily. And when she looked at the wall at the picture glass, it looked quite empty, as if a mirror hung there, not a picture after all. She slid down again, buried herself in bed, huddled the blankets round her, trembling, but not only from the cold.

For a while she might have slept again. What stirred her next was sound; a creak, footfalls. Emily, she thought, in huge relief, out of bed, hence the empty bed, now coming back. She opened her eyes, peering out of the covers, to find the moonlight much diminished. She did not yet want, dare, to see more, so shut them again, before they had begun to be able to decipher the rest of her surroundings.

'Emily,' she said, 'Emily, is that you?' Her voice came in a kind of croak, which demonstrated to herself, if not to anyone else, how frightened she was.

There was no reply. 'Emily?' she said again, screwing her eyes more tightly shut than ever. This time a voice came, barely discernible, making whisperings which she only began to recognize. But they were desperate, pleading, frightened whisperings.

'Ag . . .' she heard. Then 'Ag . . . Aggie. Are you awake? Aggie, Aggie, Aggie. Wake up, Aggie.'

Charlotte was digging herself into the bed, rigid all over, clutching sheets, blankets; could not, would not look.

'I'm not Aggie,' she was crying out, not knowing if aloud or in her head. 'I'm not Aggie. Go away! I'm not her. I'm Clare, I'm Clare. No, I'm not. I'm Charlotte. I'm Charlotte, I'm Charlotte.' She was screaming it at last, again and again. 'I'm Charlotte.'

The next thing she knew was Emily sitting up in bed, saying, 'Clare, did you have a bad dream or something?'

'I think so,' Charlotte said, dazed and shivering, not knowing whether it had been a dream or not. There came a knock on the door, and Miss Agnes's little whispering voice.

'Are you all right, dear? Are you all right?'

'I'm sorry. I just had a bad dream,' Charlotte explained. She was still shivering all over, and did not stop shivering till she fell asleep again.

Next day was the seance. Charlotte wanted nothing to do with it now. She was thinking such terrible thoughts, growing more frightened even than she had been in the night, understanding or perhaps fearing more. Suppose, she thought, suppose it wasn't a dream I had? Suppose I did go back again in time, and I was Miss Agnes for a little while, and it was really Arthur whispering? Suppose another time I changed with her properly like I changed with Clare? It was her room then after all, the one we're in, and maybe I'm sleeping in her bed. Suppose I grew up like Miss Agnes? Oh no, she thought, horrified. Oh *no*.

She only half believed it. So many things were different. She did not look like Miss Agnes when grown up. But by now she did not feel she could be sure of anything. The seance seemed the more dangerous, because so unknown and unknowable;

and yet eventually, almost inevitably, she let Emily persuade her to hide in the window bay. She could not help herself any longer.

The medium was a little brown dumpy woman with skirts almost to the floor and a hat like a basin, pulled well down. Except for a purple wispy scarf about her neck she looked as indeterminately round and ordinary as a loaf of bread.

'I thought she'd be different from that. I thought she might wear special clothes, you know, like fortune-tellers do.' Emily sighed disappointedly as they waited hidden in the alcove behind the brown velvet curtains.

'Perhaps she's got better clothes on underneath her coat, and we'll see them when she takes it off,' Charlotte suggested.

But the medium took off nothing save her gloves, revealing podgy shapeless hands with a plain gold band on the wedding finger, instead of the amethyst or topaz or turquoise rings both Charlotte and Emily thought would be appropriate. Her hat hung over her eyes like continuous brows, from under which she peered morosely. She did not smile and almost did not speak, seeing the room set out as matter-of-factly as a doctor or lawyer arranging a consulting room.

The dim side lamps were unlit today. The centre lamp was pulled right down over the table, which normally stood beside Mrs Chisel Brown's armchair near the fireplace, to hold her photographs. Now moved to the middle of the room, it held only one photograph, a large one of Arthur in uniform, at which Charlotte looked with interest from between the curtains, her face and mouth pressed to their thick and yielding pile. Arthur's face was set as sternly as in the photograph upstairs, but did not wear the same grimace. His eyes gazed out as if they passed the photographer without noticing him. The moustache was different too, clipped very neat and small.

The medium sat down at last, folding her hands over her fat brown bag, and beckoned to Mr and Mrs Chisel Brown to do the same; for though it was their house they seemed uncertain, hesitant. They lowered themselves silently, and afterwards Miss Agnes came forward and took the farthest chair from Charlotte and Emily, the one that faced them across the table. She twisted her fingers together nervously and twisted and turned her head. She touched her throat sometimes with a gesture that

Mr Chisel Brown also used for touching his moustache. The medium gazed at Miss Agnes for a minute; and then suddenly she turned and gazed at the curtains behind which stood Charlotte and Emily. Charlotte felt as if her eyes stared straight into the medium's beneath her basin hat; but the medium's face changed not at all, remained quite blank and still. After a moment she turned back to the table, to the light, to the three Chisel Browns, and, setting her bag beside her with a surprisingly large sound, she laid her hands out flat on the table. She nodded to the others and they did the same, so that there were eight, flat, starfished hands.

Nothing happened for a long time. Emily fidgeted and sucked the curtains and sighed with such loud sighs that Charlotte thought she would be heard. She herself wanted to cough. The velvet tickled her nose, and one of her feet started to go numb. Her eyes swam with gazing at the light. It felt like gazing into the bright centre of a dim flower, the opposite of a sunflower, the hands like part of the flower, not part of the people.

Suddenly the medium spoke, making them jump after the long silence. She spoke slowly at first, then a little faster, though her voice was kept at the same flat tone.

'A . . . I get. I seem to get A . . . Does anyone here know someone whose name begins with A?'

Mr Chisel Brown touched his moustache again and nodded sharply. Mrs Chisel Brown bent her head and left it bent. Miss Agnes said 'yes' very quietly.

'A wants to get in touch with someone else – A again – is that right?'

This time Miss Agnes nodded. No one else moved. The medium sat on solidly, hunched, and for another moment dumb. Then she spoke again and her voice was changing, becoming deeper, fuller, faster, if still as monotonous.

'I have a message from A . . . to A . . . to Ag . . . Agnes – is that right? All right, all right, all right. Aggie, soldier, soldiers, soldiers – no soldiers, eyes blind – *Aggie*.'

The three Chisel Browns were watching the medium, eyes fixed, faces tense. Charlotte realized she had never before seen Mrs Chisel Brown concerned about anything except food.

Again there was a pause, a long one, seeming longer at such a time.

The voice returned, deeper but getting higher, shriller as it went on. 'No soldiers, no soldiers, Aggie, eyes blind, eyes blind, Aggie, Aggie, *Aggie*.'

Miss Agnes leaned forward. She cried out, twisting, twisting with her hands. 'Arthur, Arthur, is that really you?' But at the same instant the voice began to die to a mutter, an incoherent mumble. 'Eyes blind, eyes blind . . .'

And suddenly everything had changed. The medium became rigid, staring, and remained so for a long moment, her round back straightened. Then all at once she started to shiver, to shake, like a wall shivering in an earthquake. Sounds were coming out of her very fast, but no words or no words they could comprehend. Charlotte found herself choked on the pile of the curtain, gripping and staring, scarcely bothering any more to keep herself fully hidden.

The sounds turned into a regular panting, the movement became a regular rocking back and forth. A voice came, quite high this time, a child's voice or a girl's.

'Emily,' it cried. 'Emily, Emily, Emily, where are you? There's so much noise, Emily, *Emily.*'

Emily had cried out before Charlotte could stop her and was running out into the room.

'Clare, oh, Clare,' she called, her voice excited at first, then almost immediately desperate. 'Oh, Clare, where are you, Clare?' Coming face to face

with the dumpy medium, she stared at her un-
comprehendingly and burst into tears – turning
back uncertainly to Charlotte and seeing only
Charlotte, crying more bitterly than ever and
rushing out of the room.

# CHAPTER EIGHT

ALL that night and day Charlotte was full of remorse and guilt. She thought she had forgotten or rather had not bothered to remember how wretched Clare must be away from her own time without even an Emily to confide in. Also she had let herself be lulled by Emily's apparent casualness into thinking she did not mind too much about the real Clare's being gone, and so had not spent nearly as much time as she should have done in thinking of ways for them to change back again to their proper times. She thought hard now to make up for it. She thought all night and day but found no ideas she had not already had, and none of them any good.

That Sunday was one of the unhappiest days she had ever spent, much worse even than the first days at Flintlock Lodge. Everyone seemed so unhappy. It was a grey, sooty, drizzling day, and the evergreens in the garden were black with rain. In the morning Charlotte and Emily were called by Mr Chisel Brown for a ceremonial lecture on how disgracefully, how deceitfully they had behaved, hiding in the alcove. But the lecture contained no proper fire, nor was Emily even faintly rebellious at receiving it. Having cried most of the night she now scarcely spoke at all.

At lunchtime no one else spoke either, except Miss Agnes who swam up from her own gloom to an occasional jarring brightness that cheered no one, least of all Miss Agnes. It made Charlotte feel even guiltier, because their seance had been spoiled by herself and Emily.

After tea Emily said, 'I'm going upstairs to bed now.'

'Shall I come up with you?'

'I think I'd like to be by myself, if you don't mind,' replied Emily in a remote, polite, unfamiliar voice. Charlotte would not have minded going to bed then herself, for she felt heavy and sleepy after so little sleep the night before. However, she felt obliged now to stay downstairs in the dining room playing patience without interest. A short time later Miss Agnes came and they played ludo together, which as a game of chance, not skill, was suited to their heavy minds that day. Miss Agnes looked like someone drowned.

'That voice,' she said at last, in a tone that veered uncertainly between a whisper and a cry, 'that voice – was it a friend of yours, Clare?'

'Well, sort of,' Charlotte said.

'Who's passed over, of course?'

'Well – yes – sort of,' said Charlotte again, for it was true, if not quite in the sense that Miss Agnes meant. 'I'm sorry we spoilt it for you,' she said in a rush. 'I'm awfully sorry. You might have heard more from your brother if it hadn't been for us.'

'I'm not sure, dear,' said Miss Agnes, in a voice that was little and tight and precise. 'I'm not sure I wanted to hear very much more. To tell you the truth, dear, I had not expected to hear anything. I'm not such a believer in spiritualism myself, but Mother insisted we have a seance here. She was so very upset about dear Arthur's death.'

Miss Agnes shook the dice and threw a six and so set another counter on its way. No more was said for the moment. But later she added, in a similar voice, 'To tell you the truth, dear, I was pleased not to hear more. I was, well, a little afraid of what he might have to tell.'

Charlotte could not think why Miss Agnes should have been afraid but did not like to ask. So she said nothing. And in a while she stared at the ludo board and not at Charlotte at all.

'Arthur always wanted to be a soldier, you know, he always wanted it, he dreamed of battles, oh, I've told you both so many times and you saw the books he had, you saw the stories that he tried to write, didn't you, Clare, dear? And you know he climbed the monkey-puzzle tree. I told you that. He was always doing things like that, dear Arthur, he was so brave and foolhardy. But then did not know how to finish what he began. That day he climbed the tree he climbed right to the top and could not get down, he could not move, he clung to the trunk and cried, even on the ground I could see him crying. He cried and cried and cried. And he was so angry with me for seeing it, he would not speak to me for days.'

'How did he get down in the end?' asked Charlotte across a long silence. She was thinking that Arthur was like she was after all, for she had done that herself, got to the top of trees and then been afraid to move. But she had not thought Arthur was like her.

'A ladder, the gardener. It was all quite safe. But I'm not trying to tell you about the tree, Clare, dear. Though why you should want to hear, come to think of it . . . I don't know why I'm telling you, it's a past story. You don't really want to hear it, do you, dear?'

Charlotte did not know what Miss Agnes wanted her to say – yes, no, or neither. She did not even know what Miss Agnes wanted to talk about. In the end, thinking, she said nothing again and Miss Agnes went on talking regardless, hesitating at first, but quickly growing faster.

'Well, it was like that, like the tree. He joined the army, I told you, dear, and I'd never seen him look so happy as the day he joined up, marching in his office clothes, with his hat and umbrella with all the other men; not smiling, very stern, but so happy, I could see. And so it was too, all the time he trained, he was happier, he said, than he had been all his life, serving his King and country. But when he went to France it changed. I could scarcely recognize him when he came back on leave for the first time. I couldn't persuade him to tell me why, to tell me everything except about the mud.

'Next time it was still worse. One night I'd heard him cry out in his sleep and when I went in to his room, he was awake but trembling, trembling, and he said, Aggie, Aggie, it was so terrible I could not imagine, and he was afraid he might run away if he went back, and they shot people who ran away. The guns were so noisy, he said, and asleep or awake he kept on hearing them when there were no guns. He broke down. He said he could not, would not go back. I said he must, of course, and he knew that too, and of course he did go. After that night he did not even suggest not going, he did not mention it.

'Then, when he went, I waited and waited. But no letter, no news came, nothing till the telegram to say he had been killed.'

'But the *letter*,' said Charlotte. 'You had that letter to say he had been brave, from the Colonel, you said.'

'I believe, dear, they send such letters anyway. To spare relatives' feelings, so it is said.'

'Well, I don't *believe* he wasn't brave. I don't believe it.'

'Dear,' said Miss Agnes stiffly, growing pinker in the cheeks, her hands tight and trembling, 'dear, of course he was brave, Arthur always was, even if afraid. Now is it not your turn to play? It is really getting to your bedtime now, and I've been talking much too long – and such nonsense too.' At which she shook the shaker wildly, so wildly that the dice skidded out, across the table to the floor, where both of them crawled to look for it, flustered, apologetic but glad of the diversion, in a way.

In the bedroom, Emily had taken all the marbles from the solitaire board, put them in a glass tooth tumbler and filled it up with water. She had set the tumbler on the table between their beds and now sat on her own bed, gazing at it. After all this time she had not even undressed herself; indeed she still wore her outdoor coat as they used to in their bedroom because it was so cold, without heating of any kind.

Charlotte went over and gazed with Emily. The marbles looked huge in the tumbler, huge and shiny and defined. But they looked part of the water too, as if by some alchemy it had formed itself into solid bubbles, these veined with colour, not reflecting colour, like soap bubbles.

'Why did you do that?' she asked Emily. 'Put the marbles in water, I mean?'

'I just felt like it.' Emily added defiantly, 'I think they're pretty. Stones look prettier under water. I didn't see why marbles shouldn't look prettier too.'

'I think they're beautiful,' said Charlotte. 'And how huge they look.'

But when she put her fingers into the water and pulled a marble out, it was small by comparison with those still in the glass, and unimportant too. It was like the difference, for instance, between Arthur's image of war and his experience of it. It was like other times, her own and Miss Agnes's proper childhood times, that seemed so near to her memory and yet so far away. It was like everything that made you ache because in one sense it was so close and in another unobtainable. Charlotte picked up the glass, held it to the light and gazed into it obliviously. For that moment everything else around her, everything else that had happened, seemed to splinter in her head and fall away.

'Hey,' cried Emily crossly. 'Hey, what are you doing? That's mine.'

'They're not your marbles,' Charlotte pointed out, still gazing. 'They're Miss Agnes's marbles.'

'It was my idea to put them in water. Give them to me.' Emily leapt up, suddenly frenzied. Charlotte had already lowered the glass in order to set it back on the table, when Emily snatched at it. The water slopped dangerously, the glass hung between hands for a fraction of time before falling with a crash to the floor. Marbles rolled everywhere with little hollow sounds. Emily and Charlotte trod on water and wet glass and looked at each other, dismayed.

They cleared the glass first and mopped the water up as neatly as they could. Then they hunted for the marbles. The floor was so uneven that they rolled everywhere, were caught in the cracks of floorboards, wedged between pieces of furniture, hidden under beds and in the corners. Wood grain patterned their hands as they crawled about, little draughts of air from under the door drilled their ears and faces. Charlotte was lying flat, reaching under a bed, her hair catching on the springs, when Emily said near by in a small cold voice, 'Of course, you're not really a bit like Clare.'

'What? *What?*' asked Charlotte, peering out.

'I said you weren't really a bit like Clare.'

'I never thought I was,' said Charlotte, not quite truthfully. 'It was you that said so.'

'You're not a bit like her. Clare wouldn't have let me listen to the seance last night. She's much too honourable, she's much too stern. I wish you hadn't let me either.'

'So do I,' cried Charlotte. 'Oh, so do I. You're not the only one.'

# CHAPTER NINE

AT eleven o'clock on a grey and gloomy Friday morning the armistice came, announced by guns and bells. The school bell added itself almost immediately, summoning everyone to the assembly room. There Miss Bite addressed them in her usual stiff manner. The war, she said, was an example for their sex. It had been won by and for such women as she hoped all of them would in time become.

'You girls,' she said, 'will grow up in a different world. Women have proved their worth not by such foolish tricks as throwing bricks through windows and chaining themselves to railings, as did some misguided women before the war, but as doctors, soldiers, sailors, as administrators and civil servants, as drivers, postwomen, shopkeepers and policewomen. The vote is no longer to be denied you now, nor your value as English citizens. So let all of you,' Miss Bite declaimed, 'let all of you grow up to be worthy of this trust, to take your place and play your part as your fellows have done in the course of a just and noble war.'

All this was very stirring and impressive. Most, including Charlotte, were impressed, but no doubt rejoiced more at the concluding announcement: that the rest of the day was to be a holiday. Only Charlotte and Emily, who had nowhere to go home to but Flintlock Lodge, did not much rejoice.

In the streets there were already signs of celebration. Boy scouts charged by on bicycles, furiously ringing air-raid alarm bells. People leaned from the open tops of buses, cheering or waving flags, or banging tin trays or ringing more bells. One man had a huge bell, twice the size of the school bell, from which they expected as huge a sound. But it must have been cracked, for it had no ring, no resonance. It made only a dull, small, thudding sound.

In their road were no buses and scarcely any people. Flintlock Lodge was so gloomy and quiet, no one might have heard the news at all, except

Miss Agnes, who apologized for the lack of excitement.

'Mr and Mrs Chisel Brown are elderly, of course,' she said, 'and peace will not bring Arthur back, so you would not expect them to be as pleased as younger folk.'

She offered to take Charlotte and Emily for a walk but at this, Emily made faces at Charlotte, nudging her, and as soon as they were out of earshot in the garden, she burst out: 'Well, I don't know about you, but I'm not going. You can go for a walk with her if you like, but I'm going across the river to see what's happening in the town, so boo snubs to you and utterly squash.'

She was lit up and excited. She ran round the house and out of the drive before Charlotte could say anything and went on running ahead of her till they reached the bridge, both very out of breath and Emily triumphant.

'There, I knew you couldn't stop me,' she said. 'Now let's go and see what there is to see.'

It had begun to rain gently. There was nothing here except the grey, empty river and the grey, empty allotments of the deer park on the far side of it where grass had been before the war, and would be again by Charlotte's time. There were ugly little sheds and fences everywhere and rows of cabbage and potato plants; these mostly just withered yellow leaves and jagged yellow stalks, reminding Charlotte of the stumps of trees in the brown magazine photographs she had looked at sometimes at Flintlock Lodge when there had been nothing else to do; remote, brown pictures of the battlefields of France.

As they came towards the gate that led out of the deer park they heard music. Through the bars of the gate they saw movement too, but could scarcely believe in what it seemed to be, until they pushed the gate open on to the street, a little cul-de-sac leading down from the main road. For there, unmistakably, stood a shabby barrel organ, with an old man at its handle dragging out a confusion of notes. There, two old women danced stiffly to the tune the notes added to, round and round and round.

They wore long black coats and long black shirts. One of them, who laughed, had a man's cap jammed straight across her head, with a hatpin spiking it, and had only it seemed two teeth, brown stumps, more like little trees than teeth. The other revealed no teeth at all, if she had any, her mouth clapped shut and sloping inwards from nose and chin. She wore a strange black bonnet like a crest, fixed on with strings beneath her chin. Its line across her head showed scarcely more sign of hair than her mouth showed signs of teeth, yet she hopped and danced with the greater energy, though the other's face was livelier.

The old woman with the cap grabbed Emily, the old woman with the bonnet grabbed Charlotte, and they found themselves, astonishingly, dancing too. Charlotte was rigid, scared by such an alien clutch. She was conscious of the harsh cloth of the old woman's sleeve beneath her hand, of the sour smell of it wafting to her displeasingly as they turned about. Emily, on the other hand, appeared unconcerned, laughing, jumping furiously. The old man turned the handle of his barrel organ faster and faster, the notes plopped out faster and faster, they danced faster and faster, twisting, twirling round. Ever afterwards Charlotte had the impression that at the height of it the old woman with the bonnet let go her hand, and so flung her right into the middle of the hurly-burly crowd that passed along the main street at the end of the cul-de-sac, though the road had been far too long for it to have happened in that way. She remembered looking back as the crowds took them on. The barrel-organ tune had slowed by then, for the two old women danced stately as courtiers and as expressionless. But she could not hear the music any more.

Then all to Charlotte seemed like a dream. She never knew if she'd dreamed or had really seen a lorry full of yellow girls – yellow faces, hands and caps and overalls. It was like being in a river, holding things dry above her head, only it was mind and sense she tried to hold, not clothes. It was like having a prison round her of coats and backs and uniforms. She was buffeted and bodiless, as if so many sensations made it impossible to isolate any.

She might have been floating, not walking, along. The crowd might have been floating too. It swayed like a moderate sea, all the faces making waves that broke and joined and fell apart again.

Charlotte began to realize how wet she was getting. Her hair had come loose from its plait and swung like whips about her face. The noise began banging at her head, the bells and drums and whistles, the dominant motor horns. Nothing was silent – people, traffic, houses. The traffic sprouted myriad arms, all waving flags or banging instruments.

The houses leaned over them with windows like opened mouths, belting out music from gramophones. Only Charlotte felt she made no sound. But when the crowd reached the town hall, a stout red ornamented place, it stopped and waited, and gradually, as voices joined voices, the singing began to merge until everyone was singing 'God Save the King', Charlotte and Emily too.

Despite all her efforts, Charlotte was submerged now in the feeling of it, mind as well as body. She felt small shivers run up and down her spine. She was neither Clare nor Charlotte any more, but one piece only of the singing, victorious crowd. After the Mayor had spoken from the town hall balcony, his voice as little as a pin from such a height, she linked hands with Emily and someone she did not know, sang 'Land of Hope and Glory' and then 'Auld Lang Syne', swaying back and forth, the movement as potent as the song.

The rain had almost stopped. As dusk fell, lights began to jump from windows all about. Up till now, though hemmed in, jostled, banged, Charlotte had been more excited than fearful, the crowd's warmth and friendliness carrying her along. But suddenly it did not seem so warm and friendly. Its edges splintered, it broke to ragged gaps where people danced. And when there was singing again it came in spurts, in dashes, one song against another, and none of them 'Land of Hope and Glory' or 'God Save the King'. Men climbed on windowsills, on to the horse trough by the town hall steps. Some inevitably fell in. Charlotte and Emily could hear loud splashes, laughter, angry voices too. Emily also laughed, hysterically, Charlotte thought. Faces seemed to leer like masks, the light part dim, part bright, catching half-faces, noses, eyes or teeth, never all at once. She felt herself pushed about, first one way, then another, in the crush of people all straining to see what was happening where they were not, their flags brandished now like spears or swords. All round her men loomed tall as towers.

Above the din of voice and instrument, Emily screamed, 'Clare, I want to get out! Oh, please take me out of here.' She had been clutching Charlotte more and more tightly, the clutch jerked at and tugged by the movement of the crowd, but at that moment someone pushing right between them broke it altogether – and when Charlotte turned to Emily she saw no sign of her. She called frantically, her voice tiny in this din. She pushed and wriggled and kicked and knocked, but every time she saw a gap and pulled herself into it the gap was sure to close. She squirmed between legs and bodies, said, 'Please, oh, please,' many times, uselessly – 'Oh, please, let me through.' But it was not a question of people moving aside for her, only of her ability to hammer out a way between them, the pleas just a concession to her ordinary good manners. Terror for Emily destroyed the timidity she would usually have felt.

'Mind out, there. Hey, hey, what do you think you're doing!' The voices battered at her, the shadows jumped, the light around broke furiously. But she was out, free at last, gasping and crying in the air, tears pouring down her face not rain, and still there was no sign of Emily. She wandered among the fringes of the people, not wanting to plunge into the crowd again, as that she judged would not help at all. She stood on tiptoe or bent down to look between legs, crying out, 'Emily, Emily,' dazed and horrified, too dazed to realize how remarkable it was that she actually found Emily again so quickly. For suddenly Charlotte felt a tug at her back, and when she turned about there was Emily. Tears marked her face but she stopped crying the moment she saw Charlotte; became more indignant than frightened.

'Why ever did you let me go like that?' she asked. 'I thought I'd never find you.'

For a while they walked around in quieter streets, up the hill and along the terrace, where also walked sad-looking, solitary men with lighted cigarettes that made little red stops in the dark. Then they went home on foot. It was quite different from their last street walk at night with its mysteriousness and sense of separate life. There had been no light then other than the moon, but now street lamps were lit and windows had no blackout blinds nor were most curtains drawn. The lights of the city made the sky glow, like a bowl placed over a candle flame.

Of course there was a row, an enormous one. That night they were sent straight to bed, but the following morning were spoken to severely and sorrowfully by several people, including Miss Agnes, who had been hurt, not to say worried by their disappearance. Charlotte felt bad about her, being quite fond of Miss Agnes by now. She herself as the elder, received chief blame for what they had done – but for once she did not mind, the result of their adventure being the best thing that could possibly have happened to them. For, though it was Saturday morning, she and Emily were sent to school to see Miss Bite, who spoke to them more severely and sorrowfully than anyone and told them in her distant steely way how disappointed she was and shocked by their behaviour. Had it not been for their motherless state she would even have considered expulsion. In any case, she could no longer trust Clare and Emily Moby to behave themselves in lodgings, had informed Mr and Mrs Chisel Brown to that effect and would now take them back to school to be closer to her eye. So many girls had been sent home with flu, she said, that there were spare beds in almost every dormitory.

After such a solemn interview, Miss Bite would certainly have been surprised, and even more shocked, to see Charlotte and Emily hug each other joyfully as soon as they were alone, neither ashamed a bit, though Charlotte usually shamed so easily. For surely, they thought, it would be only a matter of time now before Clare and Charlotte would each be in their own times again.

At Flintlock Lodge Mrs Chisel Brown appeared as indifferent to their going as she had been to their coming. Mr Chisel Brown, however, seemed to have regained his fire, all his puffed-out look, listing to them, through Miss Agnes, every one of their misdeeds, both those they knew about, for instance Emily's cheekiness on saying goodnight, and their invasion of the seance, and others that Charlotte had not been aware of committing, such as leaving his newspaper untidily folded and treating unkindly the hairy little dog.

Only Miss Agnes was sad. She had seemed to avoid them in their disgrace, to be rather stiff and embarrassed, even lowering her eyes from them at mealtimes. But as they were due to leave, she came up to their room a little furtively and stood in the doorway, her thick brows knitted, her cheeks pink. In her hands she held her own silk-clad doll, Arthur's box of soldiers, the solitaire board and the cloth bag that held the marbles. Dear Charlotte, she knew had liked the doll, dear Emily the soldiers, and both of them had liked playing solitaire, whereas doll, soldiers and solitaire were quite wasted on herself and on Mr and Mrs Chisel Brown. So she wondered if Charlotte and Emily would care to accept them as gifts in memory of their stay at Flintlock Lodge. They were not, though, to mention this to either Mr or Mrs Chisel Brown.

'Don't they know you're giving them to us?' asked Emily, naughtily. 'Would they be cross?'

Miss Agnes blushed and giggled. She wore a frilly blouse, the frill copying unkindly her uneven line of teeth. 'Of course, dear, I would not give you these things if they were not sure to agree them appropriate. Come and see me, dear,' she said to Charlotte pleadingly. 'I shall miss you – both of you. I did enjoy talking to you – reminding myself of . . . of . . . Oh, please come. Please come.'

Charlotte promised she would, but uncomfortably, since she hoped so soon to be back where visiting Miss Agnes would be quite impossible. The real Clare would have nothing to say to Miss Agnes in her place.

'I bet Mr and Mrs Chisel Brown didn't know about us having those things,' said Emily afterwards. 'I bet they didn't really know.'

# PART THREE

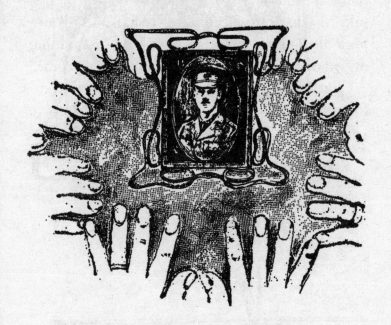

# CHAPTER ONE

CHARLOTTE and Emily were put together into the same bedroom, though they had expected to be separated. Still better, they were put into Oaktree, the largest room in the school. It had eight beds, and one of them belonged to Bunty who was subdued somewhat since her father's death, but only by her own standards, not by anyone else's. Ruth was also there, recovered from flu. She had been at home for some time, convalescing, so Charlotte had not seen her since the night she had climbed into the school. She tried to avoid her now, blushing at the thought of it, trying to imagine what Ruth might say. But Ruth rushed over to her especially.

'Do you know, Clare,' she cried, 'do you know, when I was ill I had such a funny dream. I dreamed I woke up and you were standing there, and you looked so real it might really have been you. Wasn't that *funny*?'

'Yes, wasn't it?' said Charlotte, blushing still more, but much relieved, the thought of Ruth having pursued her uncomfortably for weeks. It was good to go to bed that night without the picture called 'Mark of the Beast' glaring at her so horribly. It was good altogether to be going to bed back in the school. The lightness and joyfulness she felt made her aware of how worried she had been, and how heavily the worry had sat upon her. Suspense and uncertainty still remained, because, although at school, Charlotte was not in the right school bed, and such a mixture of feelings made it hard for her to sleep that night.

Elsie Brand slept in the same room. The ending of the war seemed to have lessened no one's dislike of her – perhaps her being half German had been after all merely an excuse. Certainly she was the hardest person to like that Charlotte had ever met, though she tried her best. One trouble was that Elsie never seemed to notice any difference between friendliness and enmity, responding to neither.

Much of the time she was ignored. But sometimes the others teased her, jointly or singly. Two nights after Charlotte and Emily came back to school Elsie had only just slipped the ribbon and slide from her long plait when Bunty, rather excited for some reason snatched both from her and threw them on to the grass roof outside their room.

The roof, over a big veranda, sloped downwards; but under their window and along the wall its top was flat and about three feet wide. Bunty and the others had often boasted they could walk on it, but it did not look particularly strong, and no one much wanted to plunge through to the stone floor beneath, so no one till now had done more than talk.

Elsie stared at the window for a moment woodenly. Then she slowly moved and leaned out of it, looking for her ribbon, which the weight of the slide had taken far beyond arm's reach.

'Why don't you go out and get it, Elsie?'

'She wouldn't. She couldn't. All Germans are cowards, didn't you know?'

Charlotte said indignantly, 'Of course Elsie isn't a coward. How can you be so beastly?'

Elsie said nothing; stared on, dumbly, helplessly at her ribbon.

'Well, she is a coward unless she goes out and gets her ribbon. It's her ribbon, after all.'

'Cowardy cowardy custard,' shouted Emily. 'Cowardy cowardy custard.' She seemed to be taking her mood from Bunty, was very loud and over-excited. 'Cowardy cowardy custard,' she cried, making Charlotte extremely angry. She too, cried out. 'Elsie isn't a coward. She isn't. You'll do it, won't you, Elsie, walk out there? And I'll come with you to keep you company.'

Somehow after a scramble they were both on the glass roof, Charlotte ahead, Elsie following, dazed-looking, as if she had been floated out on Charlotte's rage, and did not know where she was, let alone why she was there. Charlotte was still angry, beginning to be frightened, but also exhilarated. Looking down through the blurred, tinted glass was like looking down into the sea. The shapes of heaped old chairs and tennis nets might have been rocks or weeds or fish. The air felt cold as water on her face. When she turned her head she saw that Elsie was white now, her face curiously flat-looking, edgeless even. Charlotte began to urge her along, to help to calm her own rising fear. The fury which had got her out on to the roof still made her forget to be as frightened as she would normally have been.

'Come on, Elsie, look, it's all right, the glass is quite strong. It must be or it would have cracked by now.'

The glass looked like ice, but felt much smoother to walk upon and less cold, if icy enough to bare feet, which grew to a point of ache when left more than a moment in one place. Sometimes her feet met the thin raised hump of the leaden joins, which felt more impressive to feet than they looked to eyes. Hands scraped along warmer, rougher brick.

Ahead, where the roof began to slope, the ribbon blew about a little on the glass. Charlotte, leading, bent to pick it up, very slowly and gingerly, but even so, as she pulled herself up again, she swayed briefly, grabbed at air, the breath lurching in her till her hands returned to the comfort of the brick. For a moment she stood to regain her calm. Then she gave the ribbon to Elsie and they both began edging carefully back the way they had come, left hands to the wall now instead of right. In front of them the heads of Ruth and Bunty poked from the window anxiously. Immediately before Charlotte's eyes Elsie's untied plait unravelled a little and blew towards her in the wind. So near safety, Charlotte became terrified at last.

'Elsie, are you all right?' she asked, with a small shake in her voice, which she could not prevent. 'You'll have to get in first. I'll wait.'

Elsie said nothing. She scarcely moved herself but was heaved by the others over the sill, her feet tilting, her skirts tumbling up.

Then it was Charlotte's turn. She gave her hands to Ruth and Emily and pushed with her feet. In her relief she must have pushed too hard because the glass immediately exploded behind her – her head jerking round she had the impression of seeing it crack, the crack spreading rapidly, as if someone invisible was drawing a line across it. Then she too, tumbled forward into the room. The soles of her feet remained so cold for several minutes afterwards they might still have been clamped to the glass.

Charlotte was very contrite next day. She had been well scolded for an action so stupid and dangerous and did not need telling how serious it had been.

'Honestly, I'm sorry Elsie,' she said, 'making you do something so silly. It was very silly of me. I don't know what came over me, honestly. Well, we got your ribbon back, anyway.'

'It didn't matter. I had another ribbon,' Elsie said.

Emily said to Charlotte, 'Clare wouldn't have done that.'

'Wouldn't she? Wouldn't she really?'

'She'd have stood up for Elsie. She might have got very angry. But she wouldn't have done anything suddenly like that. Clare doesn't do things suddenly. Sometimes I get awfully cross with her for being so cautious. It's not that she isn't brave, of course,' Emily added in a rush. 'She's fearfully brave.' There was silence briefly. Then she said, even faster, so fast that Charlotte only just caught what she said, 'I'll miss you, honestly I will, though I want Clare back.'

'Will you?' Charlotte blushed with pleasure and delight. 'Will you really, Emily? But I'll miss you too.'

'Of course you'd rather have Emma than me, wouldn't you? Because she's your sister.'

'Yes, she is my sister,' said Charlotte cautiously. It would be lying to say she would not take Emma, if she had to choose, but she had grown extremely fond of Emily, besides not wanting to hurt her.

'Well, Clare's my sister, isn't she? But I think I might miss you all the same,' said Emily, in her funny abrupt manner, and giggled off, as if it did not matter what she said. She reminded Charlotte suddenly and painfully of her own sister Emma.

If Miss Bite had intended at first to show extra strictness to Charlotte and Emily – and even more when the roof was broken – this turned out impossible. Not only more and more girls but more and more teachers too, were going down with flu, and the teachers left spent much of their time in the sickroom, helping Nurse Gregory. The sickrooms were crammed, and there seemed little hope immediately of Charlotte's departure. But once in the school she was prepared to wait a while, and so apparently was Emily.

Charlotte was surprised enough by her own patience. She thought it must be because now within reach of her own time she felt apprehensive about returning to it. So much would have happened that she would be expected to know about, but did not know; and there was no one to help her in that time as Emily helped her here. Also she was so used to trying to behave like Clare that she could not remember what it was like to behave like Charlotte. She scarcely seemed to know even who Charlotte was. What Emily had said after she had fetched Elsie's ribbon from the glass roof had encouraged her only for a little while.

This was altogether a strange separate time; the fog had closed down outside, making the school even more than usual a little separate box-like place with its own pleasures and concerns. No grass, no trees, no streets, no traffic were to be seen beyond its walls, only the yellow, flannelish wall of fog.

School became like a game, a picnic, because of the fog, the ending of war, the flu. Lessons were improvized in the day. They did more dancing than history or arithmetic, the dancing mistress being well, the other ill. In the evenings they were able to play wild games, piling all the mattresses on the floor in their bedroom and jumping from the tall white cupboards; playing leapfrog, backs bent the length of the long room; playing Sardines and Murder in the Dark, bodies squashed into the big white cupboards, unseen but creepy, suffocatingly heavy and warm. No one came near to find them out, except one night when the murder victim screamed too loudly, too realistically, and brought Nurse Gregory running in.

Charlotte for this little while was happier than she had ever been in Clare's time; warm and contented. She almost wished it would go on for ever, that nothing would change at all. When the chance came for her to return to her own time, if it ever did, she was afraid she might have been gone too long and that if she did sleep in the bed with the little wheels the magic would not work again. Perhaps it was the same contentment and the same fear that made Emily patient too; but Emily did not say.

The chance arrived at last, so calmly and easily it seemed odd that it had never come before. Emily caught the flu and went to bed. After three days a note was smuggled from the sickroom by someone just recovered. It was written on a piece of exercise book paper, rubbed and grubby and folded so minutely it took Charlotte a frustratingly long time to unfold.

*I'm in the room,* it said. *Next to the Bed. It will be empty tonight. If no one else gets flu. Better come tonight. Love, Emily.*

For the rest of the day, despite pleasure and excitement, Charlotte was overwhelmed by a huge and melancholy nostalgia. That night happened to be her bath night, and she lay in the miserly inches of lukewarm water she was allowed, listening to the gaslight fizzling on the wall, holding in her hands a cake of brown, translucent soap. With the help of its glum and parsimonious smell she was trying to fix it all in her mind – how the past looked and sounded, at its wartime bleakest as at its best. This room, partitioned in her own time into a row of narrow bathrooms, was still one big room with a row of baths, each with a curtain round it. Behind the next curtain she could hear Bunty splashing and singing; even Nurse Gregory's voice, sharp as glass, telling them to hurry and dry themselves – even that seemed something to cling to and regret.

In bed Charlotte put hairbrushes on her pillow, one on each side of her head, to stop herself falling asleep. She did sleep once, but rolling over grazed her cheek on the prickles of the brush and awoke startled, but half dreaming still, imagining a hedgehog in her bed.

There was a little gleam of light through the glass panel above the door. In a while she could see enough to climb out of bed, put on her dressing gown and creep out of the room without knocking into anything.

The passages were as long and empty as they had been before, the light as dim. The strip of matting down the centre felt unfriendly to her bare feet, yet Charlotte only vaguely noted it, for, creeping along, she had begun to realize properly that she would never see anyone again, Bunty or Ruth or even Elsie, unless, of course, she saw them grown-up. She heard Nurse Gregory's footsteps once and the clatter of her starched clothes – more sounds she would never hear again, if the bed was empty, if its magic worked.

Inside the sickroom she thought for a horrid moment that the bed was not empty, that someone was lying there, but it proved only a rounded shadow after all. The bed awaited her, and so did Emily, still wide awake.

'I thought you were never coming,' she whispered accusingly, as Charlotte groped her way across the room, stubbing her feet painfully on the iron wheels of the bed.

'I went to sleep by mistake. I put hairbrushes by my head, though, and they woke me up all right.'

'Thank goodness for that,' said Emily, in a heartfelt voice which hurt Charlotte a little, although she had felt the same herself.

'Other people have slept in your bed,' Emily went on, 'and they're always just the same in the morning. So it must be something special to do with you and Clare.'

Unless the bed doesn't work any more, Charlotte thought but did not say. She asked instead, 'Are you better, Emily? How's your flu?'

'Oh yes, they say I'll get up soon, I haven't had it badly at all. I'm glad, I'm sick of this bed, and Gregory's horrid powders, whatever they are, and medicines.' After a long pause Emily added anxiously, 'Aren't you ever going to get into bed?'

'Oh yes, of course,' cried Charlotte, who had been standing beside her, so agitated that she climbed into bed wearing Clare's dressing gown.

'If you shout like that,' Emily was whispering severely meanwhile, 'you'll wake everyone up and then Nurse Gregory will come, and then where will you be?'

But no one in the other beds had stirred. Emily and Charlotte lay in silence for a long time. Charlotte felt so wide awake she wondered if she would ever fall asleep. What would happen if she stayed awake all night and did not sleep? Would the magic, could it, happen then? She almost believed that nothing would happen in any case. Her own time seemed so remote and unlikely now. And it was only belatedly that she remembered she must say goodbye to Emily.

But Emily's breath was even, slow. She was asleep. Charlotte wanted to wake her, to say goodbye, but it seemed unkind. In a rush of difficult, muddled feelings she began to cry, stupidly, sadly, burying her head in the increasingly sodden pillow and wondering as she cried what would happen if Nurse Gregory came in the night to find her in this bed. Then, unexpectedly, she too, fell fast asleep.

# CHAPTER TWO

CHARLOTTE was woken suddenly by a sound that bewildered, even terrified her, before she realized what it was: an airline directly overhead. She had forgotten about airliners. Her pillow was now not damp, but she was still wearing Clare's dressing gown.

'Goodness, Charlotte, whatever did you go to bed in your dressing gown for?' Susannah asked her curiously. She did not notice the other dressing gown lying at the foot of the bed, and Charlotte thrust it hastily in a drawer, wondering if Clare would be in trouble for having no dressing gown. But it was not a thing she could ever find out; any more than she could find out if Clare had got back to her room safely or been found in the bed beside Emily.

Whenever Charlotte looked up she saw Elizabeth staring at her hard. In the washing cubicle she went on staring, until suddenly her face slipped and she grinned. Charlotte grinned back at her uncertainly. Elizabeth looked untidier, more lumpish, than ever, her hair wild from the night.

'You're back,' she said. 'I wondered when it would happen.'

'I'm *what*?' asked Charlotte, pretending uncertainty till she could be quite sure.

'Back,' said Elizabeth. 'Instead of Clare,' she added, Charlotte still standing silently.

'How did you know?'

'I'm so brilliant, of course. Well, I guessed. At least, I guessed something was funny, I guessed it, oh, for ages. I asked Clare, like I asked you, and in the end she told me. Actually, I think she was quite pleased. It must have been awful for her, anyway, and much worse if no one had known anything, all the time.'

'I'm glad you knew. I'm glad. I had Emily, her sister, you know, and that helped me a lot.'

In fact Elizabeth's knowing helped Charlotte, helped smooth out the difficulties she had expected, though it did not stop the odd fuzziness she felt, the confusion at the change. In a way it depressed her that no one else had noticed that she had replaced Clare.

'Was Clare very like me then?' she asked Elizabeth one day, cautiously, because still quite shy of her, as well as of this particular question. She was hoping that Elizabeth would answer no, just as she had once hoped Emily would.

'No, really. No, I don't think she was.'

'Well, why doesn't anyone notice then?'

'Anyone would think you wanted them to,' said Elizabeth. After a while she added, 'I tell you who in this school Clare did look most like and that's Sarah, Sarah Reynolds. You know, the one Vanessa calls Lady Sarah.'

So might Clare look if she had been Sarah's mother, Charlotte thought confusedly. She had been folding a jersey of Elizabeth's, but let it drop upon the bed and stood for a moment, still and dazed and quiet.

'Was Clare like me otherwise?' she went on insisting. 'I mean, did she do things like me? What ways were we different, Elizabeth?'

Her need was to define herself, Charlotte, as much as Clare. She needed it enough to keep on badgering, uselessly.

'Well, she used to fold my clothes up just like you do. Look.' Elizabeth was suddenly exasperated. 'Look, Janet and Vanessa are a bit alike, aren't they, and do things alike sometimes, though they're quite different really? But would you be good at explaining why they were different, just like that?'

'No, I suppose I wouldn't be.'

'And at least they're both here at once, but I've only seen you and Clare separately.'

Gradually Charlotte slipped back into normal living. People no longer looked at her in a peculiar way because she asked the wrong questions or gave the wrong replies. Teachers had got over their surprise because she had suddenly become so much worse at netball, but so much better at English. All that was left to her of the past was the nostalgia she felt at unexpected moments, when she found coal-tar soap in a bathroom or one day at tea time when they were given Chelsea buns which had been one of the few nice things to eat in Clare's time. Bunty and Emily had used to try to make them last as long as possible, unwinding them carefully and picking out the currants one by one.

Yet all this while Charlotte still had not talked to Sarah Reynolds. Partly she did not know how to start – it seemed impertinent to question a prefect about her mother, whatever the excuse. Partly she was almost afraid of the answers she might get. So she did not ask her questions. If anything, she found herself avoiding Sarah so as never to have the chance of asking them. She might have gone home at the end of term and still not have known what she wanted to know, if her form mistress had not been ill one morning and the register called instead by an elderly teacher, partly retired, who came two or three times each week to take special classes in geography. Charlotte had seen her. But she had never known the name of this small woman with her bright eyes like an elderly bird, and her manner that tried to be gay. She wore her waists tight, as if she had once had more hip to curve below – indeed her clothes all looked to have more stuff in them than her shape now needed. She wore a black velvet ribbon in her hair. Vanessa and her friends played her up a little, but not too much, for she had some authority. They giggled behind desk lids now and then, and answered with voices louder than necessary when their names were called.

Vanessa's hand waved suddenly. The teacher was talking to Susannah and did not notice her at first.

'Miss Wilkin, Miss Wilkin,' called Vanessa, waving her hand more furiously than ever.

Charlotte did not at once take in the name. Then, a moment later, gasped, jumped, stared unbelievingly.

'*What*'s her name?' she whispered, nudging Elizabeth.

'What? Who? Oh, her. Miss Wilkin,' said Elizabeth, her mind elsewhere.

Charlotte stared at this Miss Wilkin, stared and stared and stared. The Miss Wilkin she had known in 1918 must surely be too old to teach, even part-time like this. Perhaps it was another Miss Wilkin. Wilkin, after all, was not such a very uncommon name. But then she remembered seeing her skip upstairs like a schoolgirl, not like a grown-up woman. Bunty and Emily had thought it funny and giggled afterwards, but it made Charlotte think now that Miss Wilkin must have been very young as teachers went, perhaps no more than ten years older than Emily herself.

Gradually, she began to see in this old Miss Wilkin the younger one; the way she batted her head about and smiled, the jolly eyes, the inappropriately nipped-in waist. On her left hand there was an engagement ring. What would Emily look like now,

Charlotte wondered sadly. In a way she wished as she had wished before, that Clare and Emily had lived long enough ago to be quite safely dead.

Not long after, on a December day, the juniors were sent for walks in groups of five or six, each in the charge of a prefect. Charlotte, Elizabeth and Susannah found themselves with Sarah, who walked them briskly to the park, over the river and up the hill. It was fine and sunny when they set out, but by the time they reached the track that led to the ponds at the park centre a smooth sheet of black cloud had come up behind them, catching the sun. A little wind had mounted too. Soon the cloud had reached over their heads and beyond. Some short and graceless trees stood here and there and to these they ran as the rain began, the wind, suddenly huge and furious, making it tear across the bracken stalks in angled veils and sheets, pushing the rain so hard round the trunks of the sheltering trees that they could stand behind them in little dry passages while everything about was drowned.

Charlotte found herself sharing a tree with Sarah. She did not look at her at first. She stood as close up to the tree as she could, rubbing her fingers on its small uneven ribs and letting herself be frightened by the wind, quite pleasurably – because so comforted by the tree. She was also thinking of Miss Wilkin and willing herself to ask Sarah what she wanted to know. They could not have been more alone and private in that wild wind and rain. But whenever she dared look round, Sarah was smiling, simply smiling, not even at Charlotte especially, which disconcerted her, and still for a long time she did not speak. Then Charlotte saw behind them a line of light beneath the cloud, drawing nearer, broadening. The rain would stop quite soon and the chance be lost. In a panic she blurted the first words out.

'Do you remember – once – about your mother? Do you remember – you told me . . . ?'

'Yes,' said Sarah. The rain still fell, but straighter, dabbing at their shoulders, patterning the earth about their feet.

Charlotte hurried on desperately.

'You said she'd told you to be nice to me, if I came – I mean, if girl called Charlotte came. And I didn't know why, because I didn't think I knew your mother.'

'Do you think you do now?'

'I was just thinking perhaps I did know her after all, only I'd forgotten, and I wondered what her name was, you see.'

'Mrs Reynolds.'

'No, I knew. I mean, what I wanted ...'
Charlotte was blushing, more and more confused.
'I mean, her Christian name. I wondered if ... Is
it ... ?' She almost said Clare, the name ready on
her tongue to echo Sarah, though it did not quite
come out. 'Do you mind my asking?'

'Of course not. Her name is Emily.'

'*Emily*!' said Charlotte at last, thunderstruck.
'Emily! Not Emily! It can't be Emily!'

'It's an old-fashioned name, but not as odd as
that.' Sarah was laughing at Charlotte now, but in
puzzlement.

'No, no, I don't think it's odd. Of course not ...
It's just ...'

The rain had stopped now, or very nearly. The
others were coming from behind their trees,
walking across towards the track. Charlotte
looked uncertainly at Sarah, and though Sarah
did not move took the chance to escape from their
conversation, marching off over the rough and
sodden earth. Sarah followed, caught her up at
once. They remained still separate from the
rest. When once Susannah seemed about to join
them, Elizabeth grabbed her arm and pulled her
back, making a wild sign with her free hand as if
to tell Charlotte she guessed what might be

happening. The other three girls remained with their heads together, farther up the track.

The sun came. It made garish, deep, deceptive colours; made the tumbled bracken bright as red earth. Charlotte thought she even saw red earth – not bracken at all – and her eyes took minutes to correct themselves. Near the ponds there was a group of trees with sick green trunks, but their twigs and branches were glowing red, as if they shed their own light instead of taking it from the sun. The ponds were a harsh battleship colour. Their blue-grey water had white flecks in it like wave crests but solider, for these were seagulls, they saw, drawing nearer, seagulls bobbing in the swell that the furious wind had raised. The wind had come so suddenly and now was gone.

Charlotte and Sarah stood by the water for a minute. Sarah bent and hurled a stick. Then they turned away across a bleakness of earth and bone-like grass, where even the sun could scarcely raise a colour. Charlotte had recovered by now from the worst of her surprise. She was screwing herself up to ask more questions.

'Did Emily – your mother – did she have a sister called Clare?' She was embarrassed enough now to have asked almost anything.

'She did, as a matter of fact. I'm called after her. My second name is Clare. But how did you know? She died a long time ago of flu. It seems odd, someone dying of flu. It was just at the end of the First World War, so my mother said.'

She spoke so casually that Charlotte would never have known what had been about to come. How can she be so cool, so calm, she was thinking, how can she be? – forgetting that to Sarah it was all past history, so long ago – that Clare was someone she had never known, only heard about.

'Charlotte, what's the matter? Whatever is the matter?'

It had taken some minutes even then, for the story to sink fully into Charlotte's mind; but, suddenly she had soaked it up and in new, full grief she had begun to cry.

On that bleak track, the sun almost gone again, tears were pouring down her face. She was crying and crying for a girl who had died more than forty years before, whom, in any normal world, to any normal way of thinking, she could not possibly have known; whom she had never even seen, though she had lived as her. She was crying for herself, perhaps, and for Emily.

*

'I think Sarah must have thought I was crazy,' she said next day. She had turned off Elizabeth's transistor and dragged Elizabeth to a bathroom and locked the door behind them. She had not wanted yesterday to speak to anyone about it, but now today she did, having woken curiously feelingless. Elizabeth was huffy as well as upset about it.

'You wouldn't talk to me yesterday, would you, not at all? I know you were miserable, but you could have said what happened. I *liked* Clare, I knew her.'

'I'm sorry. I'm awfully sorry,' Charlotte said. 'It was so sad. I didn't know what to do. Don't you mind too?' For Elizabeth seemed so much less grief-stricken than Charlotte had been, although picking a sponge to pieces all over the bath.

'Yes, I do mind. I do mind. It makes me want to cry. But it's so long ago. It's all over. She was a sort of ghost really, wasn't she? But I know it can't seem so long ago and gone to you.'

'I suppose I must have been a sort of ghost too, in 1918 – if you can have ghosts from the future.'

'She was a pretty solid sort of ghost, of course, if bony. You could feel her bones and they felt hard as yours or mine. You couldn't put your hand through them like you're supposed to with ghosts. Of course, it might have been more interesting like that.'

Charlotte shuddered. 'Suppose I hadn't been able to feel my own bones. That would have been horrid.'

'Interesting though,' insisted Elizabeth. Charlotte said, tentatively, because this fear had been so deep in her that it seemed dangerous to reveal it even now, 'Do you know, do you know, I was afraid of one thing? I was afraid I wasn't going to be able to get back here, and then I thought I might – Sarah's mother – might be me, grown up.'

'But you couldn't have been,' said Elizabeth. 'You'd have had to be alive twice over, I mean, little as Charlotte and then grown up as Sarah's mother, Clare. I don't think that would be possible.'

'I used to think ghosts weren't possible,' said Charlotte.

Elizabeth almost shouted, hands flying, face red, 'But look, of course! Don't you see? That's why Clare couldn't have been Sarah's mother either, because she'd have to be alive twice at the same time, as you and her – I mean, Sarah's mother.'

'You mean,' said Charlotte, aware for a flash what Elizabeth was saying, though afterwards her brain dull again, 'you mean . . .'

'I mean Clare could only come into the future, into now, because she died – because she isn't alive now.'

# CHAPTER THREE

IT was late now, near prayers. They rushed back to their room to find Vanessa and Janet, tight-lipped and righteous, making a bed each, Susannah, her expression a copy of theirs, picking up Elizabeth's clothes. Charlotte was apologetic, but not Elizabeth, who bundled clothes into heaps and into her already scrambled drawers, enraging everyone more than ever. But it was she who ceased to be communicative for the rest of that day, shut behind a book. This left Charlotte with time to consider everything they'd said, and so it was she thought of Miss Agnes again. If Elizabeth was right she could not have changed with her as once she feared she might, because then Miss Agnes would have been alive twice over in 1918.

Arthur was dead, though. She must have heard his ghost in the dream that time. Charlotte believed in ghosts, for after all, she had been a kind of ghost herself. Indeed, she could believe in almost anything happening now.

'It doesn't explain everything,' Elizabeth said later. 'Why it happened to you particularly. Why no one else changed, sleeping in that bed.' She and Charlotte were alone in the bedroom, sitting on their beds. 'You were quite alike, I suppose, I mean both of you having no mother, and having younger sisters and just starting school. Oh, and then both of you happening to sleep in that same bed.'

'There were the dates too,' Charlotte remembered suddenly. 'You know, the dates were on the same day of the week – I mean Saturday the fourteenth then was Saturday the fourteenth here. I should think that might have helped as well.'

'It doesn't seem enough,' said Elizabeth doubtfully. 'It must have been a chance in a million; what happened, I mean. You are *lucky*. I wish something like that would happen to me.'

'Do you?'

'Why, aren't you glad it happened?'

'I suppose I am.'

Charlotte was leaning against the bedrail fingering its shape. She touched the bedknob, tried a preliminary twist. But it did not budge.

'It used to unscrew,' she said vaguely, not particularly concerned. Yet twisted harder, using both her hands. Still she could not shift the knob at all.

'Here, let me try,' said Elizabeth, and took the knob in her own shapeless but powerful hands. Once, twice, she failed too. But the third time, with grunts from her and a grinding of rust from the metal, the knob turned and came away in her hands.

'It's hollow,' she said reflectively, peering down into it. In sudden, unexpected frenzy Charlotte pushed her hands away. 'Let me see, let me *see*,' she was saying frantically.

And at first she thought there was nothing there at all. For the book had been pushed right down out of fingers' reach. They only got it out in the end by unbending a wire coat hanger and flattening its hook and pulling it out with that. It emerged rather crumpled and torn at the bottom, the pages by now somewhat yellowed, the ink brown; Clare's thin wartime exercise book of more than forty years before.

Charlotte sat with it in her hands, hardly daring to open it. She expected perhaps, or at least hoped for, one final message from Clare, that she had not read before. It would have seemed conclusive, appropriate, even a little comforting. Instead she found only a message from herself, written the day before Clare and Emily should have moved to lodgings, the day she had expected never to change with Clare again. To see her own handwriting brown with age was almost the greatest shock of all.

'Goodbye, Clare,' her letter ended. 'Good luck. I'll never forget all this. I hope you won't either. With love from Charlotte.'

All the remaining pages were blank.

Two days later the parcel came. No one had sent Charlotte a parcel at school before, nor did she expect anyone to, so she did not bother to look at the list that went up each morning on the noticeboard. She did not look that day. It was Vanessa who shouted it along the passage.

'Charlotte, you lucky thing, you've got a parcel.'

It sat in the matron's room, and had been opened, as all school parcels were. There were several smaller parcels inside; little round things grinding in a leather bag, something round and flat wrapped in tissue paper, a box with hard shapes each wrapped in more paper, the tissue soft and yellow.

The bag had marbles in it, and the round flat thing was the solitaire board. In the box were some soldiers, their paint almost all flaked off. There was a letter, too in a mildly scented envelope.

'Dear Charlotte', it said.

*I did not send these before because I wanted to make quite sure you would get them, not Clare. I wanted you to have them though. Miss Agnes gave them to both of us after all, and I think I've had my turn! I'm afraid, though, I couldn't bear to let you have the doll. It was so like the one my mother had, which got lost, unfortunately, a great deal of time ago.*

*Did you know Clare had died? If so, I hope you didn't worry too much what had happened to me (like Clare you used to worry a great deal too much). Of course, it was a terrible shock, but more than forty years ago now, a long time. Clare caught flu not long after she returned: had it very badly for some reason and died about four days later. Many died of flu that year you know. I stayed at the school for six years, but went home every holiday to our Aunt Dolly, and my father joined us permanently when he was demobilized, so I grew up very happily, though missing Clare. Then I got married and had four children, in spite of what I always said – which shows, I suppose, that one's views change.*

*One thing I never quite knew was when exactly you would come to the school. If you and Clare ever mentioned the year, I did not remember it, but I hoped one of my girls would coincide with you; this being Sarah's last term, I had rather given up hope, so I was delighted when she wrote to tell me a Charlotte Makepeace had arrived. Of course she does not know why I am interested in you.*

*Her name is Clare, did you know? Her second name only. Her father preferred Sarah. She's not unlike my sister Clare.*

*I was strongly tempted to come down to see Clare, but did not dare. Nor do I think I could face seeing you. (Or perhaps I could not face your seeing me.) I'm quite plump and grey now. To me it feels extraordinary that I should be old enough to be your grandmother, having once been your younger sister. (Odder still to you, I should think, since you are still a child.)*

*When I was little I used to think each birthday*
*that now I should catch Clare up, forgetting she*
*would have birthdays coming too. In a way, I*
*suppose this is fulfilment of a dream, gone mad.*

*With love, yours,*

*Emily (Reynolds).*

Charlotte had locked herself in a bathroom to
read this letter. After a while she unlocked the door
and took the packages back to her own room. She
hid the solitaire board under some clothes in her
drawer, but put the marbles in a glass tumbler,
which she filled up with water and set on her chest-
of-drawers. She put the lead soldiers to flank it
on either side. The marbles looked very pretty,
everybody said, and Charlotte was pleased, because
no longer now was her chest-of-drawers the only
one without an ornament. It looked individual. It
belonged to someone. It seemed odd that it belonged
to her more as Clare than as Charlotte. But she had
begun to realize that she could never entirely escape
from being Clare. The memory of it, if nothing else,
was rooted in her mind. What had happened to her
would go on mattering, just as what had happened
in the war itself would go on mattering, for ever.

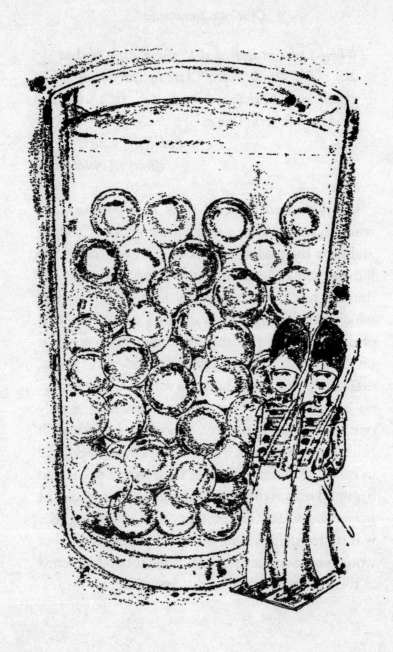

A PUFFIN BOOK

# Extra!

## Extra!

## READ ALL ABOUT IT!

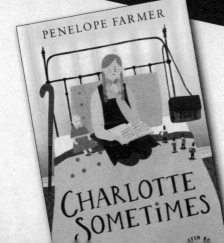

PENELOPE FARMER

CHARLOTTE
SOMETIMES

| | |
|---|---|
| 1939 | *Born 14 June in Kent*<br>*Attends boarding school*<br>*Reads History at St Anne's College, Oxford* |
| 1960 | *Her first collection of short stories,* The China People, *is published* |
| 1962 | The Summer Birds, *her first novel for children, is published. It is the first book of a trilogy featuring the characters of Charlotte and Emma Makepeace* |
| 1963 | The Summer Birds *receives a Carnegie Medal commendation and is cited as an American Library Association Notable Book* |
| 1966 | Emma in Winter, *the second book featuring Charlotte and Emma Makepeace is published* |
| 1969 | Charlotte Sometimes, *sequel to* The Summer Birds *and* Emma in Winter, *is published* |

| 1972 | A Castle of Bone *is published* |
| 1977 | Year King *is published* |
| 1989 | Thicker than Water *is published* |
| 1993 | Penelope: A Novel *is published* |
| | *Lives mainly in London* |

## INTERESTING FACTS

Penelope was a twin, although her parents and doctors weren't aware of her existence until she was born twenty-five minutes after her sister.

In 1981, English rock band The Cure released a song with lyrics inspired by the book which was titled 'Charlotte Sometimes'.

Penelope Farmer has written for children and adults all her life. *Charlotte Sometimes*, her most popular children's novel, has never been out of print.

# WHERE DID THE
# STORY COME FROM?

Charlotte Sometimes *was inspired by Penelope
Farmer's own family and people that she knew. The
characters of Emma and Charlotte are based on her
mother and her aunt, and the story is drawn from
the many tales Penelope had heard about the schools
her mother had attended. Penelope also used her
own experience of boarding school life when she was
growing up at the time of the First World War.
A familiar background made it easier for her to
frame the story and develop the plot.*

# GUESS WHO?

**A** *He had white hair, white brows and a white moustache struck across his bright red face, like a Christmas parcel with white ribbon round it.*

**B** *She was tall, smart and stoutish, and wore pink-rimmed spectacles and pink lipstick and usually suits of tweed. She had a jolly smile, inviting confidence.*

**C** *It wore a blue silk dress short to the knee and humped a little behind, tied by a pink silk sash, also a hat with a feather in it. It had laced high-heeled boots painted on its legs, and impossibly tiny feet.*

**D**

*'Wake up, dreamy,' a voice prodded at Charlotte from the other side of the table; a surprisingly deep imposing voice, for it belonged to a small round girl with spectacles and with black hair cut quite short instead of long in a plait like most people's. She had also a very snub nose.*

**E**

*. . . the way she batted her head about and smiled, the jolly eyes, the inappropriately nipped-in waist. On her left hand there was an engagement ring.*

ANSWERS: A) *Mr Chisel Brown* B) *Miss Bowser* C) *Miss Agnes's doll* D) *Bunty* E) *Miss Wilkin*

# WORDS GLORIOUS WORDS!

*We often come across **new** or **unfamiliar words** when we're reading. Here are a few unusual words you'll find in this Puffin book. Did you spot any others?*

**Stoutish** *Bulky in figure; heavily built; fat*

**Séance** *A meeting at which people try to make contact with the dead*

**Conchies** *Short form for conscientious objector, a person who refuses to join the army because they think it is morally wrong to do so*

**Convalescing** *Recovering one's health and strength over a period of time after an illness*

**Impertinent** *Rude and not showing respect, especially towards someone older*

**Lodgings** *Temporary place to stay*

# QUIZ

**1** *What did Charlotte find on the chair next to her bed instead of her new book?*

a) *A little prayer-book and a shabby Bible*

b) *A navy cardigan*

c) *A doll*

d) *A blanket*

**2** *What is the name of the Chisel Brown's house?*

a) *Aviary Hall*

b) *Flintlock Lodge*

c) *Cedar Cottage*

d) *Monkey Gardens*

**3** Which poem did Charlotte recite in Miss Bowser's class?

a) *Boadicea: An Ode*

b) *Brook*

c) *Mark of the Beast*

d) *How Horatius Kept the Bridge*

**4** Who threw Elsie's ribbon on to the glass roof outside?

a) *Charlotte*

b) *Emily*

c) *Bunty*

d) *Ruth*

**5** What was not in the parcel Emily sent to Charlotte?

a) *A doll*

b) *Marbles*

c) *Lead soldiers*

d) *A solitaire board*

ANSWERS: 1) *a* 2) *b* 3) *d* 4) *c* 5) *a*

# IN THIS YEAR

## 1969
### Fact Pack

*What else was happening in the world when this Puffin book was published?*

American astronauts Neil Armstrong and Buzz Aldrin become the first humans to walk on the Moon.

Sesame Street first appears on television.

The first human eye transplant is performed at Methodist Hospital in Houston, Texas, USA

Concorde, the world's first supersonic airliner, makes its first flight.

*English explorer Sir Wally Herbert is the first man to walk across the Arctic Ocean and reach the North Pole on foot.*

*The 50p coin is introduced.*

# MAKE AND DO

Clare used a war-time exercise book as her diary. She and Charlotte wrote messages for each other and hid the diary in the hollow bed post of their bed. You can create your own secret diary easily too!

*Create your own secret diary!*

## YOU WILL NEED:

* A notebook

* Cardboard for the front and back cover

* Coloured paper, fabric or stickers for decoration

* Ribbon

* A small lock and key

* Sticky tape and clear glue

* Scissors

* A ruler

* A pencil

1   Measure and cut two pieces of cardboard to fit the front and back cover of your notebook.

2   Cut two pieces of ribbon each measuring roughly six centimetres.

3   Fold one ribbon in half to make a loop. Secure with sticky tape or glue on to the long edge of the front of your notebook. Make sure the ribbon loop sticks out slightly over the edge to hook over your lock.

4   Do the same with your other ribbon on the back.

5   Decorate both pieces of cardboard with coloured paper, stickers or fabric.

6   Stick your decorated cardboard paper on to the front and back of your notebook.

7   Hook the lock on to the loops of your ribbon and you have created your own secret diary!

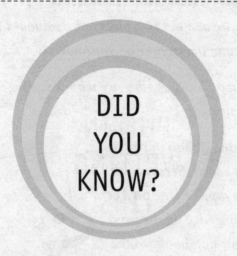

# DID YOU KNOW?

The First World War, also known as the Great War, was the first war to be fought by every major power in the world.

Women were employed in large numbers to do jobs left unoccupied by the men who had gone to war. They worked as doctors, sailors and policewomen etc., and they enjoyed the independence and opportunities.

Soldiers would spend their time in the trenches fulfilling their duty, firing at enemies, doing chores, playing cards and writing letters home.

Goldfishes were placed in the rinsing water to test if gas masks still had poison on them after washing.

Girl Guides were used to carry messages containing sensitive and confidential information for the British Secret Service MI5.

# PUFFIN WRITING TIPS

*Watch the news and stay tuned to the latest happenings in the world – you never know what might inspire your next idea.*

*Write a letter every day, even if it's only a very short one! Think carefully about who you're writing to and how the letter should be written.*

*Listen to your favourite piece of music and then write about what you imagine as it plays.*

*Keep a travel journal when you go on holiday so you can capture all the exciting new sights and sounds.*

A PUFFIN BOOK

### Animal tales

☐ *The Trumpet of the Swan*
☐ *Gobbolino*
☐ *Tarka the Otter*
☐ *Watership Down*
☐ *A Dog So Small*

### War stories

☐ *Goodnight Mister Tom*
☐ *Back Home*
☐ *Carrie's War*

### Magical adventures

☐ *The Neverending Story*
☐ *Mrs Frisby and the Rats of NIMH*
☐ *A Wrinkle in Time*

### Unusual friends

☐ *Stig of the Dump*
☐ *Stuart Little*
☐ *The Borrowers*
☐ *Charlotte's Web*
☐ *The Cay*

### Real life

☐ *Roll of Thunder, Hear My Cry*
☐ *The Family from One End Street*
☐ *Annie*
☐ *Smith*

# stories that last a lifetime

Ever wanted a friend who could take you to magical realms, talk to animals or help you survive a shipwreck? Well, you'll find them all in the **A PUFFIN BOOK** collection.

**A PUFFIN BOOK** will stay with you **forever**. Maybe you'll read it again and again, or perhaps years from now you'll suddenly **remember** the moment it made you **laugh** or **cry** or simply see things **differently**. Adventurers **big** and **small**, rebels out to **change** their world, even a mouse with a **dream** and a spider who can spell – these are the characters who make **stories** that last a **lifetime**.

Whether you love animal tales, war stories or want to know what it was like growing up in a different time and place, the **A PUFFIN BOOK** collection has a story for you – you just need to decide where you want to go next . . .

A Puffin Book can take you to amazing places.

# WHERE WILL YOU GO?

## #PackAPuffin